Daredevi

Joe looked in the rearview mirror. Through the pouring rain, he could see the bright headlights of a pickup truck. Joe fixed his eyes in front of him. He was rapidly approaching a sharp curve and knew he would have to slow down a little to negotiate the bend.

"Brace yourselves!" Frank warned just as the sports car entered the curve.

The pickup truck with the darkened windows smacked into the rear bumper of the sports car. The force of the impact made the car swerve as it rounded the bend. Joe fought the wheel to stay in his own lane. The tires gripped the slick road just enough to keep the car from careening into an oncoming station wagon.

As the sports car exited the curve, the pickup truck smacked into the rear bumper again, this time with even more force. The car began to fishtail toward the edge of the cliff, protected only by a metal guardrail.

The Hardy Boys Mystery Stories

Available from MINSTREL Books

159

DAREDEVILS

FRANKLIN W. DIXON

A
MINSTREL®
BOOK

Published by POCKET BOOKS
New York   London   Toronto   Sydney   Singapore

This book is a work of fiction. Names, characters, places and incidents are products of the author's imagination or are used fictitiously. Any resemblance to actual events or locales or persons, living or dead, is entirely coincidental.

A MINSTREL PAPERBACK *Original*

 A Minstrel Book published by
POCKET BOOKS, a division of Simon & Schuster Inc.
1230 Avenue of the Americas, New York, NY 10020

Copyright © 2000 by Simon & Schuster Inc.

Front cover illustration by Bill Schmidt

ISBN: 0-671-03861-3

First Minstrel Books printing January 2000

10 9 8 7 6 5 4 3 2 1

THE HARDY BOYS MYSTERY STORIES is a trademark of Simon & Schuster Inc.

THE HARDY BOYS, A MINSTREL BOOK and colophon are registered trademarks of Simon & Schuster Inc.

Printed in the U.S.A.

Contents

DAREDEVILS

1 Hollywood or Bust

Fire. There was fire everywhere. Frank Hardy stole a furtive glance at his younger brother, Joe. Frank, the dark-haired older son of Laura and Fenton Hardy, was sweating, wishing he could be safe at home instead of trapped like a rat. Joe, who was seventeen and a year younger than Frank, looked completely cool.

He's drinking this in, Frank thought. He looks as if he's in seventh heaven.

Frank stared into the flames. Are we ever going to get out of here? he thought. Is this ordeal ever going to end?

Then a lone figure emerged from the flames.

1

The man—tall, with a rugged face apparent despite a coating of ash and soot—headed straight for the brothers. He paused to glance back over his shoulder at the raging inferno. Holding his hand out, he uttered the words Frank Hardy had longed to hear since he had become trapped in this building nearly two hours earlier.

"I've had enough of this heat," the man said with a toothy grin. "Let's get out of here and into someplace cool."

"I'll second that," Frank whispered. He stood up and stretched his back. "Come on, Joe."

"Wait a minute," Joe replied. "I want to see the credits."

Frank stared for a heartbeat at his brother. Then, knowing that protest would be futile, he sat back down. When the lights finally came on inside the Bayport Multiplex, Frank offered up a prayer of thanks.

"Now can we go?" he asked his brother.

"I take it you didn't like the movie," Joe said as he stood up.

"What was there to like?" Frank asked. He reached down to the floor and retrieved an empty popcorn bag. *Flame Broiled* was definitely half-baked."

"I admit the movie wasn't great," Joe replied,

"but it was just an action flick. And some of the action was really good."

"It did have some awesome stunts," Frank said as he stood. "But the plot was so thin you could see right through it." He glanced at the floor around him. "Did we pick up all our garbage?"

"Got it all," Joe said.

"I especially liked the stunt where Michael Shannon used the emergency fire hose to swing from one ledge to the other to rescue the cat," Frank said as they emerged onto the street. "But a stunt should not be the only likable part of a whole movie."

It was a hot summer day in Bayport, and though he had wished to be out of the theater only moments before, he now regretted leaving the building's air conditioning.

"Actually, that wasn't Michael Shannon in that scene," Joe said as he rooted in his pockets for the keys to the brothers' van. "At least I don't think it was."

"What do you mean? I thought Michael Shannon was one of those actors who always did his own stunts," Frank asked.

"He used to," Joe responded. "But I read in a review that the studio had brought in a stuntman because of the difficulty and danger of some of the action."

"You read a review of this movie and we still went to see it? Just for that, you ride and I'll drive."

Joe handed his brother the keys. "Ah, who listens to reviews these days?" Joe got into the van. "Anyway," he added, "that's why I wanted to see the movie credits. I wanted to see who did the primary stunts."

"Like you know one stuntman from another," Frank said with a laugh.

"Hey, some guy's job is to jump into fires, drive in high-speed chases, and fall from a cliff, I figure the least I can do is show him some respect by learning his name."

"And?" Frank asked after a moment of silence.

"And what?"

"And what was his name?"

"Oh," Joe said. "Terrence. Terrence McCauley."

Twenty minutes later Frank and Joe were standing in the living room of their home. Fenton Hardy was on the phone, and by the former police officer's somber tone, his sons could tell that something was seriously wrong.

"You're right, Brian," Mr. Hardy said into the

mouthpiece. He sat next to the coffee table, looking down at some notes he had hastily scribbled on a small pad.

Rope—cut?
Window—glass
Empty extinguisher!

"When did you get the last call?" Mr. Hardy asked. "Yesterday?" he inquired as he jotted down the words. "Two on Tuesday."

Frank and Joe gave each other questioning looks, but neither had any idea why their father was so concerned. Since retiring from the police force, their dad had been a private detective. Obviously, the conversation had something to do with a case, but what they were hearing didn't seem to fit what the two knew about the cases their father was currently working to solve.

"I see, Brian," Mr. Hardy said. "Not a problem. I owe you one anyway. I'll make the arrangements and get back to you with the details. Until then, keep your eyes peeled and keep him safe."

Mr. Hardy hung up the phone.

"Keep who safe?" Laura Hardy asked as she entered the living room. Frank and Joe's mother had become accustomed to the occasional danger the men in her life found themselves in.

"Brian McCauley's son," Mr. Hardy replied. "You remember him, don't you?"

"Little Terrence?" Mrs. Hardy was surprised. "What kind of trouble has he gotten himself into?"

"Terrence McCauley!" Frank shouted. "What a coincidence."

Mr. Hardy looked at his older son. "What do you mean?" he asked.

"We just saw *Flame Broiled,*" Frank answered. "And Terrence McCauley was the stunt double for the star, Michael Shannon."

"Stunt double," the boys' mom said. "So he followed in his father's footsteps."

"You sure have a memory for details, dear," Mr. Hardy said with a smile.

"Speaking of details, Dad," Joe said, "how about filling us in. What kind of trouble has this Terrence McCauley gotten into?"

"Well, first of all, it's not so much trouble that he got himself into," Mr. Hardy started. "It's more the trouble that somebody else wants to put him in."

Mr. Hardy sat on an armchair across from his two sons. Mrs. Hardy sat next to her husband on another chair.

"Let me start at the beginning," Mr. Hardy continued. "I know how you two like to get all the background details on a case."

Frank reached over and took the writing pad and pen from the coffee table. "Shoot, Dad," he said when he was ready to take notes.

"I met Terrence's father some twenty-two years ago while he was in New York making a movie. I was working as a detective with the NYPD. There had been a robbery near the movie set. I was chasing down the thief on foot, and without knowing it, we both ran into a building that had been rigged with explosives for a stunt in the movie. Brian saved me and the thief when the building began to crumble."

"So that's how you two became friends?" Frank asked.

"Yes," Mr. Hardy said. "We kept in touch over the years. Your mom and I even went out to visit Brian and his family in California once. We were there when . . ."

Mr. Hardy's voice trailed off. His wife reached over and gave his knee a loving squeeze.

"We were there when his wife died in a car accident," Laura finished for her husband.

There was a moment of awkward silence.

"So what's going on now?" Joe asked.

"Well, Brian raised Terrence alone since the boy was three. The first thing Brian did was quit being a stuntman. He didn't want to risk his life anymore because his death would leave Terrence an orphan."

"So what did he do?" Frank asked.

"Brian stayed in the movie business," Mr. Hardy continued. "He became a stunt coordinator."

"So Terrence grew up around action movie sets?" Joe inquired.

"Exactly," Mr. Hardy responded. "And when the boy turned sixteen just five years ago, he became a stuntman—against his dad's better wishes, I might add."

"Why didn't Brian McCauley want his son to become a stuntman?" Joe asked. "Because of the danger?"

"Brian had so convinced himself that stunt work was deadly dangerous, probably as a way to rationalize giving up the work himself, that he didn't want Terrence to be a stuntman," Mr. Hardy answered.

"So what happened?" Frank asked.

"In the end Brian gave in. Terrence threatened to move out and do it anyway. Brian realized it was better to keep the boy close at hand and try to be the stunt coordinator on some of his jobs so he could watch out for him."

Mr. Hardy stood up. "Now it seems that somebody besides his father wants Terrence to give up stunt work. He's received several threatening calls and anonymous notes telling him that his days are numbered. And there have been a few odd accidents on the sets where he's worked. Yesterday, a rope he was using snapped and he nearly fell twenty stories. Luckily, another stuntman was there to save him."

"So, where do we fit in?" Joe asked.

"*We* don't fit in. I fit in."

"Aw, come on, Dad," Joe protested. "We want to help on this case. Don't we, Frank?"

"It has been a while since we've been to California," Frank said in support of his brother. "And anyway, what is Terrence, twenty-one? We're closer in age to him than you are. We'd blend in with his crowd better, so we could keep an eye on him."

Mr. Hardy slowly shook his head at his wife. "How is it that our sons always have a good point?"

"Now, if you three think you're going off to Hollywood and leaving me here alone," Laura scolded, "you've got another think coming."

"Mom!" Joe and Frank shouted in unison.

Laura stared her sons straight in the eyes. "If Terrence McCauley is as stubborn as you two, he's going to need all the people he knows looking out for him."

"All the people, dear?"

"Yes, Fenton, all the people. I haven't seen that boy or his father in a lot of years. Plus, a summer vacation in Hollywood could be a lot of fun!"

Forty-two hours later the Hardys arrived in what was usually known as sunny southern California. This particular Thursday, however, the normally clear summer sky was filled with thick clouds as a rare rainstorm blew in from the Pacific Ocean.

The Hardys piled into the two cars they had rented and made their way to the Curtis Hotel. Brian McCauley had wanted them to stay at his house, but Mrs. Hardy insisted that six people would be a crowd and that she was looking forward to staying in a hotel.

The Hardy-McCauley reunion was not delayed, though. Terrence and his father were waiting in the hotel lobby when Frank, Joe, and their parents arrived. After the introductions were made, the McCauleys and Hardys retired to their suite so the Hardys could freshen up.

"You folks picked a good night to arrive," Brian McCauley said. "There's a big Hollywood party tonight, and we're all going."

"What party?" Joe asked.

"Mad Alliance Studios, the makers of *Flame Broiled,* are throwing a party to give the movie some more heat," Terrence said. "Have you guys seen it?"

"Yeah," Frank said unenthusiastically. Then he added, "Loved the stunt with the cat. Was that you?"

"Yup," Terrence said. "In fact, it was my cat!"

The group split into two to head for the party. Frank and Joe wanted to shower, so Brian Mc-Cauley took Mr. and Mrs. Hardy in his car to the party. About twenty minutes later, well after sunset, the younger men exited the hotel.

"I called to have my car brought around," Terrence said.

Joe's eyes lit up when the valet attendant pulled up in a beautiful silver sports car.

Under the hotel awning, Joe admired the car's sleek lines, playing his fingers across the gleaming silver exterior.

"You want to drive?" Terrence asked.

"Does he want to drive?" Frank laughed.

Twenty minutes later Joe opened the car up as

he guided it into the Hollywood hills. The rain was pouring down, making the roadway treacherously slick, but the sports car hugged the asphalt.

"Supreme handling," Joe said, beaming.

"Uh, Joe," Frank said from the car's cramped backseat, "are you slowing down?"

"Haven't touched the brakes," Joe replied. "Not going fast enough for you?"

"Not me," Frank responded, "but that truck behind us is sure coming up fast!"

2 Life of the Party

Joe looked in the rearview mirror. Through the pouring rain, he could see the bright headlights of a pickup truck. Joe fixed his eyes in front of him. He was rapidly approaching a sharp curve and knew he would have to slow down a little to negotiate the bend.

"Brace yourselves!" Frank warned just as the sports car entered the curve. There was nobody ahead of them, so Joe chose not to slow down as much as he should have. Still, the car's own speed did not prevent the impact, though it did lessen its force.

The pickup truck smacked into the rear bumper of the sports car.

"Hey!" Terrence yelled, even though the driver behind them could not hear.

The force of the impact was enough to make the car swerve as it rounded the bend. Joe fought the wheel to stay in his own lane. He didn't want to risk a collision with any cars that might be coming around the bend from the opposite direction. The tires gripped the slick road just enough to keep the car from careening into an oncoming station wagon.

As the sports car exited the curve, the pickup truck smacked into the rear bumper again, this time with even more force. Terrence McCauley's expensive dream machine began to fishtail toward the edge of the cliff, protected only by a metal guardrail.

Joe worked the brake and then the accelerator to keep the car from spinning into the barrier. The pickup truck drove up next to them.

The truck smacked the sports car on the driver's side, sending it toward the railing once again.

"Right rear!" Joe shouted in warning, calling out the spot on the car he knew would hit against the barrier. He successfully fought the steering wheel to lessen the impact. The car kissed off the guardrail exactly where Joe had planned. Unfortunately, the kiss was strong enough to catapult the car back into the lane at a forty-five degree angle, allowing the truck to sideswipe it again.

This time the impact was on the driver's side fender. Terrence groaned at the sickening crunch.

"Straight, brakes!" Frank shouted from the backseat. His shout warned his brother that he needed to stay in his lane and slow down a bit. As the pickup truck swerved into the lane just ahead of the sports car, Joe realized why Frank had called out the instructions. There was traffic coming in the other lane and Joe needed to give the pickup truck a chance to squeeze in front of them.

The two vehicles rounded another bend. Joe wanted to stop, but there was no place to pull over. As they entered another narrow straightaway, the pickup swerved into the now-empty left lane. It decelerated a bit and rammed its fender into the sports car's driver's-side door. Terrence's car began a treacherous spin as the pickup truck accelerated and sped away.

Time seemed to slow down for the three young men in the silver sports car. Joe struggled with the steering wheel. He used both feet to work the accelerator and brake, subtly changing speed to try to bring the car under control. He managed to stop the spin just enough to keep the car from hitting the guardrail with too much force. The metal rail bent out over the cliff and the front of the car crumpled, but Joe had succeeded in keeping the car from breaking through the railing, thus saving them from a deadly plunge.

"Is everybody okay?" Frank asked from the backseat.

"My shoulder hurts a little, but it's just a bruise," Terrence replied.

"My knuckles are sore from gripping the steering wheel, but otherwise I'm just peachy," Joe answered. "Steamed, but peachy."

"Man, that was some great driving, Joe," Terrence said as he unbuckled his seat belt. "You could be a professional stunt driver."

"Thanks," Joe replied. "In our line of work, it's a requirement."

"Yeah," Frank added. "But the car insurance payments end up setting us back a bundle."

"Hey, this is California," Terrence said. "My insurance rates are going to be higher than a mortgage payment after this."

Terrence and the Hardys got out of the car. "I just wish I could haul that maniac in the truck into court to make him pay for this."

Frank watched the sparse traffic whiz by.

Though every driver slowed down to peer at the scene, not one of them stopped to help. They all just went on, leaving the three of them standing in the rain next to the heavily damaged sports car.

"You'll get your chance," Frank said. "I got the truck's plate number."

"During all that mayhem?" Terrence was surprised. "Boy, you guys really are good. We'll just tell the police and let them go arrest that lunatic."

"Nope," Frank said. "We keep this info to ourselves and tell the police some truck bumped us twice and we spun out on the wet road. If the cops haul him in for this, we get him on reckless driving and your life is still in danger. We need to nail him for more than a traffic incident."

More than an hour after the "accident," the three young men arrived at the *Flame Broiled* Light-the-Fire Party. A passing motorist had finally stopped to help. The good Samaritan used his cell phone to call the police. After giving their statements concerning the incident to the authorities, Frank, Joe, and Terrence were free to go. They asked the police to phone for a cab, which took them to the Mad Alliance Studios event.

The Hollywood party was being held at Clemen's Terrace, a favorite facility of movie studio executives. Clemen's Terrace was a huge renovated warehouse, and the studios could decorate it any way they wanted. In this instance, the facility had been transformed into several scenes from *Flame Broiled,* each depicting one of the many fiery locations where the movie's primary action took place.

"Terrence McCauley!" a sweet voice called out almost immediately after the three men entered the party. "I was beginning to think that you would never arrive."

The techno-rock party music was loud, yet Frank and Joe instantly locked in on where the voice had come from. Joe tapped Terrence's arm to point his attention in the proper direction.

"Pam Sydney," Terrence muttered under his breath before the woman was in range. Joe could see that Terrence instantly became uncomfortable as the woman approached, but he wasn't sure why. Pam Sydney was pretty. She had short, raven black hair, and her round face was very animated. By the way the woman's eyes glittered as they took in Terrence McCauley, it was obvious that she was attracted to the handsome stuntman.

Pam tucked her arm in Terrence's as soon as she was within reach.

"My, I can tell by your expression that something is wrong," Pam said to Terrence. She reached up with her free hand and straightened his hair. Terrence shook his head at her touch, a bit too strongly Frank thought.

"Nothing's wrong, Ms. Sydney," Terrence said. "Nothing some body work won't fix."

Pam looked confused.

"We had an accident on the way here," Joe said as he offered his hand to the attractive woman.

"Uh, do I . . ." Pam began to say.

Terrence cut her off. "Pam Sydney, meet Joe and Frank Hardy. Guys, this is Pam Sydney. She runs Mad Alliance Studios."

"Friends of yours?" Pam asked. "A bit young for you, perhaps?"

"Good friends of mine," Terrence said.

Pam shook Frank's and Joe's hands. The handshakes were brief, and Pam quickly rehooked her arm in Terrence's.

"Your accent," Frank said. "Australian?"

"Very good," Pam replied. "Pam Sydney, from Sydney."

"Oh, look," Terrence said. He wiggled his arm free from Pam. "It's our folks," he said, pointing across the room at nobody in particular.

Frank immediately followed Terrence's lead. It was obvious to him that Terrence was trying to extricate himself from the woman.

"Oh, yeah," Frank said. "We should check in with them and tell them about the car."

"I don't see your dad," Pam said as she quickly glanced around. "You should stay in one spot so he can find you." Pam put a hand on Terrence's shoulder.

Joe could see that Pam wanted Terrence right where she had him, and Terrence, though he was attempting to mask his true feelings, wanted to put some distance between himself and the studio executive.

"Well, I see my dad," Joe said as he looked in the general direction that Terrence had pointed. "And he came with Brian McCauley, so we should report to him."

"Oh, all right," Pam said. "We'll go find your parents." She slipped her hand around Terrence's closed palm.

"Perhaps you should mingle with the press and the other guests," Terrence said. "You know, make yourself available to the media." He began to walk away from Pam.

"I guess you're right," Pam said halfheartedly. Then she recovered her smile and perked up. "I am the voice of Mad Alliance, after all." Pam headed off in the opposite direction.

When they were out of earshot, Frank gave a gentle shoulder bump to Terrence. "Using the old I-see-my-dad trick, I see."

Terrence laughed.

"What I don't get," Joe said as the three meandered toward the center of the room, "is why you wanted to ditch her. She's very pretty, and it's obvious that she likes you."

"No kidding," Terrence responded. "But I'm not interested."

"Why?" Frank asked.

"She's a spoiled rich kid," Terrence said. "She came here a few years ago from Australia with her daddy's checkbook, opened a studio, and declared herself a movie mogul."

"But you work for her," Joe said.

"Lots of people work for her," Terrence replied. "The studio produces several movies a year. She's even made some money for her dad. Not that he would care. Kyper Sydney would do anything for his daughter."

"The guy must be loaded," Joe said.

"Very," Terrence said. "He owns Mad Alliance International. They're a huge corporation with interests mainly in shipping, airlines, and construction. He gets what he wants, and Pam thinks she can have anything *she* wants."

Frank scanned the room. He had yet to spot his parents or Brian McCauley. Before he even had time to wonder if they had arrived, though, the partygoers began to applaud.

"Our illustrious guest of honor has arrived," Terrence said. Frank noted the sarcasm in the young stuntman's voice.

Blinking his eyes against the flashes of light, Frank zeroed in on the center of attention.

"Michael Shannon," Joe said as he spotted the movie star. Shannon made his way toward the front of the room, putting him just a few feet from the three young men. The star of *Flame Broiled* ascended three steps onto the raised dais at the front of Clemen's Terrace.

"Thank you everyone, thank you," he said, raising his hands in mock modesty. Camera flashes filled the air with spots of light.

"It's great to be on fire!" Shannon shouted in reference to his movie. The crowd laughed. "Now, I know I haven't done many interviews for the press lately, but with a hot movie like this, I'm willing to field a few questions."

"He's one big image, huh?" Joe whispered to Terrence.

"All image," Terrence replied as Michael Shannon answered a question concerning his next project.

As the actor quipped for the press, a tall, lanky man with bleached blond hair pushed his way past Frank.

"I have a question," the man shouted at Michael Shannon. The actor gave the man a quizzical look.

"Ian Edrich, *Slow Motion* magazine," the man said. The actor nodded his head, indicating that he would field the question.

"Thanks," Edrich said. "First, we all know that *Flame Broiled* is a turkey at the box office. Care to take the blame for this one, or are you going to pass responsibility off onto somebody else like you did with your last failure?"

The crowd became silent.

"I'd say the only turkeys are the ones in the audience who couldn't grasp the subtleties of a masterful story," Shannon replied abruptly.

"Heh, yeah," Edrich mocked. "One more thing. When are you going to give your stunt double top billing? After all, he does all the hard work."

Michael Shannon's face flushed with anger. "Why you dirty . . ." the actor snarled as he leaped off the stage.

3 Bad Press

Michael Shannon's hands were around the reporter's throat before his feet even touched the ground. He squeezed the man's neck and shook him hard.

"You filthy little liar!" he shouted in Ian Edrich's face.

Frank, who was the closest person to them, grabbed Michael's right wrist and applied pressure until the actor was forced to release his stranglehold. Michael whirled on Frank and took a swing. Frank easily blocked the wild punch.

"Who do you think you are?" Michael shouted as he readied another punch. Before the actor could aim a blow at Frank, Terrence McCauley grabbed the enraged movie star from behind.

"Michael, Michael," Terrence said. "Get a hold of yourself."

"Let me go, you wannabe," Michael spewed. He wriggled free from Terrence's grip and turned to face the stuntman. "If anyone's turned my movie into a turkey, it's you! Your easy-way-out stunts made me look bad."

"Michael, dear," Pam Sydney cooed as she stepped into the fray. She placed a calming hand on Michael's shoulder. "Manners, manners," she said. Then she cocked her head toward the crowd.

"You'll have to excuse my tired star," she said loudly. "He's been working himself very hard lately. All of us know how stress can make us act a bit silly."

Pam began to walk Michael away from the crowd. "Come on," she said, "let's get you something cool to drink." She pointed a hand at the DJ and nodded her head. "Come on, everybody," she shouted as the DJ cued up some music. "This is a party!"

As Pam Sydney led the seething actor away, Frank turned his attention to the man whom Michael Shannon had attacked. He saw that his brother was already helping the man, who rubbed his neck. The reporter was breathing heavily.

"Man," Ian Edrich said as he gasped for air, "that guy's grip is stronger than I thought it would be."

"You mean you figured he was going to attack you?" Joe asked.

"Uh, no," Ian said, glancing sideways at the teen. "I, uh, just figured that a guy who didn't do his own stunts wouldn't be all that strong."

"Stunts take skill, not just strength," Terrence said as he and Frank joined Joe and the reporter. "And I think you've overstayed your welcome." Terrence pointed a stern finger at the front door.

Ian Edrich straightened his clothes. Without a glance at the stuntman or the two teens, he began to walk toward the exit. However, Frank, Joe, and Terrence all wanted to see him out to the street. They had some questions for the reporter.

"You deliberately provoked Shannon," Joe said. "Why?"

"Hey, if he can't take a little heat, he shouldn't make movies like *Flame Broiled*. Criticism is the name of the game in Hollywood."

"True enough," Terrence said. "But you used me to set Michael Shannon off. I don't even know you, and I thought I knew all the reporters at *Slow Motion* magazine."

"I'm new," Edrich said. "Looking to make a name for myself. And, hey, I'm the reporter—I'll ask the questions."

"Ask away," Frank said.

Edrich hesitated.

"You guys are nothing," he said after a moment. "I'm not wasting my time talking to you." The reporter began to walk toward the parking lot.

"Hey!" Joe shouted.

"Ah, let him go, Joe," Frank said. "There's nothing to get from him now."

Frank then turned to Terrence. "You, on the other hand—I think there's something we can get from you."

"What do you mean?" Terrence asked.

"What's the deal with you and Michael Shannon?" Frank asked. "He went rabid at just the mention of you, his stunt double. If somebody hates you enough to want you dead, I'd say he's suspect number one."

"Michael Shannon?" Terrence sounded incredulous. "Yeah, you can say the guy doesn't like me. But enough to try murder?"

"Why doesn't he like you?" Joe asked. "Anything specific?"

"We've known each other since we were kids," the stuntman replied. "If you know a bit about his career, you know he began acting when he was nine. I was around the movie sets a lot because of my dad. He was a spoiled rich kid, I was just a poor kid to him. You could say we never liked each other."

"You know a lot of spoiled rich kids." Joe laughed.

"Here in Hollywood money equals status," Terrence said. "People sometimes forget to take you for what you're worth instead of for what your house is worth."

"Did you guys ever fight?" Frank asked.

"Verbally most of the time—physically a couple of times."

"You win?" Joe asked.

"Win, lose." Terrence scuffed his feet. "Nobody wins a fight."

"Especially when it's kids who are fighting," came a voice from over Terrence's shoulder. Brian McCauley put a hand on his son's arm. "It's not about who's stronger, it's about right and wrong."

"You taught your son well," Mrs. Hardy said as she and Mr. Hardy joined the group.

"But you and Michael Shannon are enemies,"

Mr. Hardy said. "At least in his eyes I'd say after that display of temper. I think we have to give that young actor a hard look. He has a motive, if that scene inside was any indication. To me it looks like he's blaming you for his flagging career."

"Now we need to prove opportunity," Joe said.

"Right," Frank added. "He did come to the party late. That would give him plenty of time to ditch the truck."

"What truck?" Mr. Hardy asked.

"It's a long story," Frank answered.

"Well, tell it to us back at the hotel," Mrs. Hardy said. She turned to both Brian and her husband. "Shall we?"

"Uh, could we have some cab money?" Frank asked.

Mr. Hardy gave his sons a wry smile. "I think Terrence should ride back with you and his dad," he said to Laura. "I'll go in the cab, and these two can fill me in on what happened."

The next morning the bright sun had returned, and Joe woke his brother early and hurried him through breakfast.

"Get a move on, Frank. Terrence told me if we're at the set by ten o'clock, we'll catch him filming some stunts."

29

"It's pretty cool of him to get us onto a movie set," Frank said.

"True, but it's part of our job," Joe replied. "After all, we are here to protect him."

"Where are Mom and Dad?" Frank asked.

"They already left for the set. They gave me keys to one of the rental cars," Joe answered.

"Great," Frank said. "You bring the car around and I'll meet you out front. I want to grab my laptop."

"Why do you need a computer on a movie set?" Joe asked.

"You'll see," Frank responded.

At nine forty-five Frank and Joe drove onto the Mad Alliance lot. After parking the car, they were directed to the set where Terrence McCauley was working on *Major Miners,* Mad Alliance's latest action flick. The two brothers took up a spot next to Brian McCauley and their father.

"Where's Mom?" Frank whispered.

"She went shopping. For her, this is a vacation."

"Quiet on the set!" the director yelled, signaling that they were ready to begin filming.

All their attention was directed to a fifty-foot-high scaffold. At the top of the metal tower stood a well-dressed woman and a burly guy dressed as a construction worker. The worker had one hairy arm wrapped around the woman's throat.

"Action!" the director screamed.

From his spot on the ground, it looked to Joe as if the woman had bit the construction worker's arm. Then, seeming to be startled by the pain, he pushed the woman away. She fell off the scaffolding backward and plunged toward the ground, where she landed safely on a huge inflated airbag.

"Cut! Perfect stunt." The director beamed.

"Boy, it's a good thing I knew they were acting," Joe said. "My first instinct was to race to the rescue."

"Then your instincts are way off." Frank laughed. He pointed to the woman as she began to walk toward the spot where the brothers and the two fathers were standing.

"What the—" Joe began, his eyes wide.

"Hey, good-looking," the woman said as she removed her wig.

"Terrence?" Joe was shocked. "When you were up there, I could have sworn you were a woman."

"The magic of makeup," Brian McCauley said. "Good fall, guy."

"Thanks, Dad," Terrence replied. "And speaking of makeup, I'm going to go to my trailer to clean this stuff off. You guys coming with me?"

"Sure," Frank said. "What about you, Dad?"

"Nope," Mr. Hardy responded. "I want to snoop around, maybe ask some questions. The accidents that hit Terrence last week all happened here. With Brian escorting me, I should get access to most everywhere."

"Sounds good," Joe said. "We'll hook up with you later."

The two fathers headed off in one direction while their sons headed for the stuntman's trailer.

"Wow, this is the life!" Joe exclaimed when the three young men entered the trailer. "I wish I worked in a place like this."

"Ah, this is nothing," Terrence replied. "Hey, Joe, could you unhook me?" The stuntman pointed to the back of the dress he was wearing.

"Sure," Joe said.

"Do you have your cell phone here?" Frank asked while Terrence began to change into some jeans.

"On the table," he replied. "What for?"

Frank hoisted his laptop onto a small wooden dining table. "I'm going to tap into the Department of Motor Vehicles' registration files so I can track down that license plate from last night."

"My brother, the boy genius," Joe said. He watched Frank connect a wire from his computer to Terrence's portable telephone. Frank then switched on the system and began dialing an Internet access number.

"That's odd," Frank said after a moment.

"What?" Terrence asked as he finished removing his makeup.

"I keep getting a connection," Frank answered, "but it won't hold for more than a couple of seconds."

Frank hit Redial on the cell phone. The familiar modem sounds echoed in the trailer, but after just a few pings and chirps, the phone's dial tone cut in.

"That makes four tries now," Frank said. He hit Redial once more.

"Hey, while Frank diddles with that," Joe said, "do you mind if I raid your fridge?"

"Help yourself," Terrence said. "There's some fruit and cold drinks in there. I'll take an apple, please."

"I don't get it," Frank said as his brother squeezed past the table and headed for the kitchenette. "According to my computer diagnostic program, there's some sort of interference that keeps me from getting a clear Internet signal over the cell phone."

Frank hit Redial at the same time that Joe

poked his head into the refrigerator. Again, the modem made a connection, chirps and beeps filled the air for a few seconds, and then the dial tone cut in.

"I give up," Frank said. He started to reach to disconnect the modem wire from the computer.

"Don't do that!" Joe shouted.

4 Dial E for Explosive

Experience made Frank stop. He recognized the urgent tone in his brother's voice and knew instantly what Joe wanted. Frank left the modem connected to the cell phone, and he hit Redial for good measure, somehow knowing that action was important, too.

"Talk to me, Joe," Frank said desperately. "What do you have?"

"A messy fridge," Joe replied. He opened the refrigerator door wide enough for both his brother and Terrence to see inside.

"That's a—" Terrence McCauley began. He

pointed to the top shelf, right next to a container of orange juice.

"Yup," Frank said. He hit Redial on the cell phone once more. "A bomb. A remote-controlled one, I would guess, by the way that blinking red light on the front keeps coming on and off in time with the noise from my modem."

"Wow," Joe said in admiration. "This is some setup."

"How so?" Frank asked. Suddenly the modem stopped chirping. From his vantage point at the table, he could see the red light on the front of the bomb click off and then on. Frank hit Redial on the phone, and the bomb light went dark.

"Remote control, about two pounds of explosive, and if I know my bombs, a tamper-proof fail-safe," Joe replied. "I won't be able to disarm it."

"Why hasn't it gone off?" Terrence asked. The stuntman, no stranger to danger but out of his element now, was frozen with fear.

"I figure the remote control's incoming signal is being blocked by the Internet connection," Frank explained. "The two radio signals keep blocking each other. It's pure luck that the two are tuned to the same frequency."

"Well," Joe said as he backed away from the refrigerator, leaving the door open, "our luck won't hold forever."

Frank hit Redial again. "We'd better get out of here. Terrence, open the front door. Joe come here and carry the laptop while I carry the cell phone. We need to keep the connection going."

Terrence moved swiftly to the trailer door. He twisted the knob and tugged. "It's stuck!"

"Probably barred from the outside," Joe said, scanning the room.

"That window above the bed," he said, pointing to it with his chin. "It's the only one big enough for us to crawl through."

"Well, crawl fast," Frank instructed Terrence.

The young stuntman climbed on the bed. He opened the window. "It's not going to work," he said, frustration and worry thick in his voice. "It's a horizontal slide window. There's only one pane of glass that opens."

"Then break it," Joe yelled.

Joe's tone of voice made Terrence regain his composure. Danger was a part of his everyday existence. Instinct took its place above fear, and Terrence acted accordingly.

With a lightning-fast, thunderously powerful karate strike, Terrence thrust his arm against the window, shattering the glass and opening a route to safety. He began to crawl through the narrow window.

"We can't make it through, holding the phone and computer," Joe said.

"Hand me the laptop," Frank ordered. Joe did as he was told. Frank carried the machine back to the table, hitting Redial as he did so. "Now out," he commanded.

Joe hopped on the bed and climbed through the window. Terrence helped him to the ground on the other side.

Inside the trailer, Frank hit Redial one last time. Then he sprinted the two strides between the table and the bed, jumped as if the cushion were a trampoline, and hurtled through the window. A piece of glass still stuck in the window frame cut his arm, but Frank wasn't going to let that slow his momentum. He wriggled through the window, Joe and Terrence pulling him out and to the ground.

"Run!" Frank yelled.

The three young men bolted from the trailer, but only a few feet separated them and the trailer when it exploded. Frank, Joe, and Terrence were thrown to the ground by the force of the blast, debris showering down on them.

To Joe, the rain of metal and wood seemed to

last for an eternity, though the last pieces clattered to the ground less than forty seconds after the explosion.

"Joe, Joe!" Joe felt a strong hand shake his body. He lay facedown on the pavement. The ringing in his ears muffled the voice of whoever was trying to rouse him.

"Joe, are you okay?" came the voice again, a little more clearly this time.

"Uh, a—a little dazed and confused," Joe stammered as he raised his head.

"Oh, then you're normal," Mr. Hardy said as he helped his younger son to his feet.

Joe looked around him. His older brother was sitting on the ground, dabbing at the blood that seeped through the cut on his left arm, but otherwise none the worse for wear.

Terrence McCauley was being tended to by his father. Joe could see that the elder McCauley was applying pressure to Terrence's shoulder.

"Injuries?" Mr. Hardy asked.

"I'm intact," Joe replied. He nodded toward his brother and the stuntman. "What's the damage?"

"Cut arm for Frank," Mr. Hardy replied. "A piece of wood hit his leg, and he'll just have a deep bruise. Terrence, however, is going to need his shoulder stitched up."

Mr. Hardy pointed to the burning husk of the trailer. The movie studio safety crew, a must on any action movie set, were putting out the fire with chemical extinguishers. "What happened in there?" he asked. "Gas leak?"

"Wrong number," Joe replied. His father gave him a puzzled stare. "Bomb," Joe added. "Whoever is after Terrence has really upped the ante."

"And then some," Mr. Hardy said. "You guys must have been pretty close to the blast."

"Less than twenty feet," Joe answered. He began walking toward his brother, who was just standing up. Though all three young men had been next to one another when they began to run, the force of the blast had thrown them several yards apart.

"How are you feeling?" Joe asked.

"Rattled, and my leg is throbbing," Frank answered. "The cut on my arm is actually from crawling through the window."

"How long was I out?" Joe asked.

"Four, maybe five minutes," Frank answered. "You sure you're okay?"

"I'm fine," Joe replied.

"We'll get him checked out just to make sure," Mr. Hardy said.

"If this all happened a few minutes ago, why

no cops?" Joe asked. "A boom like that is hard to miss."

"It's a movie lot," Mr. Hardy answered. "Stunt explosions happen all the time. Cops would only respond here if called."

The three Hardys walked over to Terrence and Brian McCauley.

"How are you doing, T?" Joe asked.

"I'll be good as new." Terrence smiled. "McCauley men are built tough."

"And thick headed," his father added. "Now maybe you'll ease off from stunt work for a while."

"I'm not letting some psycho scare me out of my life's work, or keep me from Daredevil Fest," Terrence said.

"Daredevil Fest?" Frank asked.

"It's a stunt competition. It starts tomorrow," Terrence replied. However, before he could explain any further, a purple convertible screeched to a halt a few feet away.

"What is going on here?" Pam Sydney's voice pierced the noise of the safety crew's fire-fighting efforts.

"There was a little extracurricular activity," Terrence McCauley said.

"Oh my gosh!" Pam cried. "Terrence, you're

hurt!" She pushed past Joe to get to Terrence's side. She stroked the stuntman's forehead.

"I'm fine, Ms. Sydney," Terrence said. "I've been hurt worse before."

Just then one of the safety crew members approached. "The fire's out, Brian."

"Thanks, Tast," Mr. McCauley replied. "Have the ambulette transport these three to the hospital."

"Hospital!" Pam Sydney screeched. "But we still have another stunt to shoot. I thought you said you were fine, Terrence."

"He'll need stitches," Brian growled.

"And they should all be checked out by a doctor," Mr. Hardy added a bit more soothingly.

"Maybe I can help," came a voice from over Pam's shoulder.

"Antonio Lawrence," Terrence said. Joe noted the veiled anger in his friend's tone.

The approaching man was about the same size and build as Terrence McCauley, no more than twenty-two years old, with short black hair and a square jaw, Joe noticed.

"A stunt get to be too much for you?" the newcomer quipped.

"Ease off, Antonio," Brian said. "You too, T."

"If you need a stunt, I'm your man," Antonio said to Pam.

"Just like you," Terrence said. "Always sniffing around other people's stuff."

"You're yesterday's side dish," Antonio said. "I'm today's main course." Antonio flashed a toothy grin at the movie studio exec.

Pam looked into the interloper's steel gray eyes. "I do need a man who's in good shape," she said.

"Then it's settled," Antonio said. "You go play doctor, Terrence, while I go help Pam."

Frank saw Terrence's body tense. He was certain that his friend was about to lunge at the sarcastic newcomer. He stepped in front of Terrence, stopping any rash action.

Antonio locked eyes with Frank for a heartbeat. Then he snorted out half a laugh.

"Let's go make some movies," Antonio said. He took Pam Sydney's hand, and the two walked away from the group.

"He's a real piece of work," Terrence began.

"Save it for later, boys," Mr. Hardy said. "Here's your ride to the hospital."

A small van pulled up to where the group stood. A paramedic—Stan, by the name patch on his blue uniform—exited the back of the vehicle.

"Won't need a stretcher," he commented. Stan pointed to the back of the ambulette. Joe went to climb in first but lost his balance and stumbled.

43

"You sure you're okay, Joe?" Frank asked as he reached out to steady his brother.

"Little wobbly, that's all," Joe replied.

"We'll order up a skull X ray, just to be safe," Mr. Hardy said, concerned.

"Well, we know that'll turn up empty." Frank laughed. He used his uninjured arm to help his brother into the back of the van.

"Ha, ha. Very funny," Joe mocked.

Frank climbed into the van and sat next to his brother. "Now we'll have proof that I got all the brains in the family."

Terrence climbed in behind Frank and Joe, being careful not to bump his injured shoulder.

"You two and all this brotherly love," Terrence said with a fake sniffle. "It's enough to make me cry."

The three young men broke out in laughter.

Ten minutes later the ambulette arrived at Gerlinsky General Hospital. It was a typically slow day in the emergency room. Gerlinsky was situated close to the posh neighborhoods surrounding the newer movie studios. Unlike inner city hospitals, which saw emergency rooms flooded with the victims of street violence, Gerlinsky General saw mostly bumps, bruises, and cuts.

Nonetheless, Gerlinsky was a well-staffed professional facility. Joe, Frank, and Terrence were attended to immediately.

Joe was sent to X-ray, and a call was put in to a neurologist to take a look at him to make sure he didn't suffer any lasting damage from having been knocked unconscious.

"I'm telling you, Doc," Frank said as Joe was led away, "you're not going to find anything!"

Later that evening the Hardys and the Mc-Cauleys relaxed at the Hollywood Hills home that Terrence shared with his father. The doctor at Gerlinsky General Hospital had confirmed that none of the young men had been seriously injured. Frank's cut had been bandaged, Joe had flirted with some nurses, and Terrence had had twenty-five stitches in his shoulder. Brian McCauley wanted the doctor to forbid his son from participating in Daredevil Fest, but Terrence protested and the doctor gave him the green light.

"So, what is this Daredevil Fest?" Frank asked. He sat on a chair across from Terrence, who was on the couch. Joe stood across the room scanning a bookshelf for something interesting to thumb through, and the adults were in the kitchen, cleaning up after dinner.

"It's this awesome stuntman competition," Terrence answered. "They hold it every year. It's a variety of tests of a stuntman's skills."

"It sounds pretty important to you," Joe said over his shoulder.

"It is," Terrence replied. "It sort of sets the pecking order among stuntmen. You know, whoever's the best gets the best jobs."

"And let me guess," Frank said. "You're the best."

"You'd better believe it," Terrence said.

"And this Antonio Lawrence wants to be the best," Frank added.

"He's a newcomer to Hollywood stunt work," Terrence answered. "He's done a lot of work in the foreign markets but not much since arriving in Hollywood last year."

"So if he wins Daredevil Fest," Joe said, still scanning the bookshelves, "he becomes top dog. Sounds like a suspect to me."

"Getting some theories together?" Mr. Hardy asked as he entered the room. He sat down on the couch.

"We have two good possibilities," Frank responded. "Michael Shannon and Antonio Lawrence. Both have a dislike for Terrence."

"Being a stuntman, Antonio probably has the knowledge and skill to pull off the attempts that have been made on T," Joe added. "And a highly paid actor like Shannon could certainly hire someone with the skill."

Just then the phone rang.

"Could I get that for you," Frank asked, pointing at the phone on the small table across the room.

"Sure," Terrence said.

"McCauley residence," Frank said into the mouthpiece. Instantly, his face perked up. He hit the button marked Speaker so everyone in the room could hear.

"You hear me!" came the disembodied voice. "If the stitches don't keep him out of action, maybe this will!"

Suddenly there was a crash. The glass in the bay window of the house shattered, and an object came whizzing into the room.

5 Fall Down and Go Boom

"Explosive!" Frank yelled as the single three-inch stick of M-80 landed four feet from him, hissing as the fuse burned down.

The Hardy brothers sprang into action. Joe hurtled himself toward the sofa, while Frank ran toward the kitchen entrance.

Like the expert football tackle that he was, Joe Hardy dove at the couch as if he were tackling an opposing ball carrier. He hit the back of the sofa between where his father and Terrence were sitting, toppling the heavy piece of furniture backward.

Mr. Hardy and Terrence flew backward, too,

and when they landed on the floor, the large wooden frame and plush cushions of the couch fell over them, protecting them and Joe from the explosion.

Meanwhile, Frank ran to his mother and Brian McCauley, who were entering the living room from the kitchen, carrying trays of drinks. The glasses they carried, as well as their bodies, flew backward as Frank wrapped his arms around them and used his momentum to hurtle them back into the protection of the kitchen just as the M-80 exploded.

Frank and Joe's lightning-quick reflexes saved everybody from injury.

"What was that?" Laura Hardy wanted to know.

"That," Frank said, "was an M-80 firecracker, as much explosive in it as a quarter stick of dynamite."

"The damage isn't too bad—the bottom of the couch is singed, the carpet's burned, but the window is totally gone," Joe said, assessing the damage.

"That's it, enough is enough," bellowed the elder McCauley as he reentered the living room, wiping iced tea and coffee from his pants. "It's time we left California for a while and let the police sort this whole thing out."

"No way, Dad!" Terrence protested as he rose to his feet. "I will not be run off like some scared puppy dog. Daredevil Fest starts tomorrow, and I am going to compete."

"Besides," Frank added as he steadied his mom, "unless you leave forever, there's no guarantee that all this won't start again once you return home. For that matter, a determined killer might just follow you wherever you went."

"Frank's right," Mr. Hardy said. After hearing the distant police sirens move closer to the house, he added, "But in any case, we're going to have police involvement now, whether we want it or not. They're on their way. It would be hard to hide an explosion in a residential neighborhood."

"Does that mean we're off the case?" Joe asked.

"Since when has police involvement ever stopped you boys from completing a case?" Laura Hardy asked.

Frank and Joe both laughed. "Then we might as well decide what to do next before the police get here," Frank said.

"I'm still voting for leaving," Brian said.

"Vetoed," Terrence responded.

"Let's divide up the labor then," Mr. Hardy said.

"Right," Joe said. "I'll stick close to Terrence, so I can watch his back."

"How are you going to do that during Daredevil Fest?" Terrence asked.

"I'm going to enter."

"What?" Mrs. Hardy was shocked.

"I'm almost eighteen," Joe said. "That should put me in the same age category as T. And since Frank is injured, I'm the logical choice."

Knowing that arguing would do no good, Laura threw up her hands in frustrated defeat. "You'd better be more careful than you've ever been," she said to her son.

"I want to finish what I started today," Frank said. "Tracking down the truck from the other night."

"And Brian and I will be at the competition to help Joe watch Terrence's back," Mr. Hardy said. "Later I might want to ferret out leads around Mad Alliance Studios."

"Great, then that's settled," Joe said.

"Hey, you're forgetting about me," Mrs. Hardy stated.

"What do you mean?" Mr. Hardy asked his wife.

"Yeah," Joe said, "what do you plan to do?"

"I'm going to try to make a new friend during the competition." Laura Hardy smiled. "Pam Sydney. From what you've told me, she has a crush on Terrence and plenty of cash to make things happen. A woman who's been rejected, especially a rich one, can make a terrible enemy."

"We'll make a detective out of you yet, Mom," Frank said.

"Make me one?" Laura responded with a laugh. "Who do you think cracks all of your dad's tough cases?"

The next morning, after hours with the police, explaining to them that the M-80 was a prank, and with a carpenter who threw up some plywood to cover the blown-out window, everyone except Frank met at the site of Daredevil Fest's first event. Frank had taken one of the rental cars to the local library to use the computers to track down the truck that tried to run them off the road on the Thursday of the *Flame Broiled* media party. The competition's first event was skydiving. Terrence had used his influence with the competition supervisors to get Joe added as a last-minute entry.

Joe and Terrence were already dressed when the rest of the gang came to wish them luck. After all the "Be careful" 's and "Go get 'em" 's, the parents went to find seats in the grandstands.

"We'd better go pack our parachutes," Terrence

52

said. The seasoned stuntman led Joe toward the long table where several other competitors were working the silk chutes into the packs.

"Big T," one competitor said, extending a friendly hand. The rugged-looking young man had a blond Mohawk. "Ready to soar?"

"You bet, Caleb," Terrence responded, clasping hands with his exuberant competitor.

"Who's the kid?" Caleb asked, indicating Joe.

"Joe Hardy," Terrence said.

Caleb offered a hand to Joe. "A little wet behind the ears," he said. "You a rookie?"

"Oh, I have some experience doing stunts," Joe replied. "I just don't get paid to do them."

Caleb laughed. "Rock on, Little Joe." Caleb picked up his packed parachute and headed off toward the competitors' trailer.

"Friend of yours?" Joe asked Terrence.

"If you're asking as a detective, I give Caleb a zero on the suspect-meter. He's a joker with a heart of gold."

"Could just be a cover," Joe said. "I've come to learn that just about anybody, friend or foe, can have a motive to do another person harm. It's an unfortunate fact of life."

"Maybe," Terrence said. "But I'll cling a little longer to my instincts. Caleb's a good guy."

"Humor me," Joe said. "Fill me in on his background."

"Not much there," Terrence replied. "His father's a pastor at a local church. Let's see, he has an older brother named Severin who's a pretty good athlete from what I hear."

"Any rivalry there?" Joe asked. "You know, something that would maybe make Caleb want to make a bigger name for himself by becoming the number one stuntman?"

"I've known this guy for a while, Joe," Terrence answered. "When he competes, it's for fun only. He wins, he loses. It doesn't faze him. He's just a bass guitar–playing, loud-talking, fun-loving stuntman."

"Ever compete for jobs against him?" Joe asked.

"Not really," Terrence said after a moment's thought. "He does a lot of key stunt work on small-budget films, stuff I don't usually touch."

"Being number one and all," Joe laughed.

"Yeah." Terrence smiled. "Being number one and all. And Caleb's a good number two or three man on big films. In fact, we worked together on *Flame Broiled.*"

"You really giving him a zero on the suspect-meter?"

"Yeah, Joe," Terrence said seriously. "An absolute zero."

Just then a short, balding man with a round face and wide eyes came trotting up to the table.

"Terrence, Terrence," he said, stepping between Joe and the stuntman, "I can't believe you're going through with this."

"What do you mean 'going through with this'?" Joe asked abruptly. If Caleb wasn't supposed to set off Joe's suspect instincts, this older man certainly was ringing the bell.

The man ignored Joe.

"I heard about yesterday," the man said to Terrence. "The explosion. I know it landed you in Gerlinsky General."

"I'm fine, Mr. Silver," Terrence said. "Thank you for your concern."

"Forget my concern," Mr. Silver said. "But how about my offer? Come on, give up this behind-the-scenes, stuntman anonymity junk. Step out in front of the camera. It pays better, and it's safer."

"Terrence," Joe said. "Mind introducing me to your friend?"

Mr. Silver glanced sideways at Joe, annoyed by his interruption. However, Terrence followed Joe's lead, sensing that he wanted to question the man.

"Joe Hardy, meet Mr. Phil Silver, head of Silver

Lining Productions. Mr. Silver, Joe's a friend of mine from the East Coast. Perhaps you might want to take a look at him if you're hoping to build up your talent pool."

"Oh, are you an agent?" Joe asked.

"Agent?" Silver seemed shocked. "Most certainly not. I'm putting together a new studio, and I need young talent with long-term potential," Silver explained.

The studio executive took a moment to stare at Joe. Joe felt as if he were being sized up.

"I like what I see, young man," Silver said. "Your good looks, obvious charm, athleticism, and your friendship with Terrence—I could use someone like you.

"As I've already offered to Terrence," Silver continued with a new smile, "I'm willing to sign a four-picture leading-man deal with him so he can give up stunt work for good. And I'm sure something can be worked out for the person who helps me convince Terrence to take the offer."

"A four-picture deal? I thought the days of studios signing actors to multimovie contracts went out in the fifties."

"They did," Silver explained. "But in Hollywood, everything old is new again. I'm looking to establish Silver Lining as a studio with longevity, not just some fly-by-night operation. To do that, I'm going to use a name-brand approach. You know, build a stable of talent that financial backers and movie patrons alike can have confidence in."

Silver turned his attention back to Terrence. "And I'm willing to make you one of my cornerstones," he said.

"Oh, no, you don't!" shouted a voice with a familiar Australian accent. Pam Sydney stormed up to the gathering at the parachute-packing table. "I want you to take twenty paces away from my man. He still has a picture to finish for Mad Alliance."

"He is not your personal property," Silver responded. "He can make your little movie the last time he has to be a nameless stuntman. I'll make him a star."

"Wow, such attention over a stuntman," Joe quipped.

"What can I say?" Terrence laughed. "Good looks and strong muscles are in these days."

"Oh, in that case," Antonio Lawrence said as he joined the group, "then they should be fighting over me."

Joe rolled his eyes.

"I was wondering where you were," Terrence said. "I was thinking you'd decided not to show."

"In your dreams, ex-champ," Antonio said.

"While you were jawing, I was strapping on my chute and posing for the cameras."

Antonio leaned in between Silver and Sydney. "You two should start bidding on me instead of yesterday's news."

Just then the verbal jabbing was interrupted by a voice booming over a loudspeaker.

"All right," the voice said, "we're ready to begin the Aerial Acrobatics Competition. The first three contestants will be Antonio Lawrence, Joe Hardy, and Terrence McCauley. Please report immediately to the airplane."

"But we haven't strapped on our chutes," Joe said.

"I guess you forfeit already," Antonio said with a laugh. The cocky stuntman turned and headed for the small prop plane that was revving its engines a dozen yards away.

"No way," Terrence said as he grabbed his parachute pack. "We'll strap in while we're climbing to the jump-point."

Terrence began to jog to the plane. "Come on, Joe," he shouted over his shoulder.

Joe grabbed his parachute and followed Terrence. He saw Antonio climb into the plane. Then Terrence handed his parachute pack to a tall, thin man inside the plane, and he, too, climbed aboard.

Joe held up his chute, thinking that somebody would grab it as Terrence's had been. However, no one reached down to take the pack. Frustrated, Joe held the pack in his left hand and reached up to the airplane's entryway with his right. He began to pull himself into the aircraft but slipped. The skydiving gear he wore was very slick, and he could not gain any leverage.

Joe tried again, and this time somebody gripped him around his arm. The grip was strong but felt weird. Joe couldn't figure out why, but he did note that the hand holding him applied a strange sort of pressure. As Joe was pulled into the airplane, he looked at the person who had aided him. It was the same thin man who had grabbed Terrence's pack. The man wore a helmet, headset microphone, and sunglasses. Joe couldn't make out his face, but he could see that the guy was the pilot.

Joe put his parachute pack down. He turned to help Terrence put on his pack, but he saw that it was already on. Joe gave the stuntman a quizzical look, but he couldn't question him over the drone of the plane's twin engines. He assumed that either the pilot or Antonio had helped Terrence into his pack.

Joe picked up his chute and handed it to Terrence, who helped him get strapped in and ready to skydive.

After the three competitors took their seats, the pilot throttled up the airplane and taxied down the runway. Ten minutes later the man signaled that they were at the jump-point. All three competitors lined up at the doorway.

Antonio was the first to jump. His wildly colored green, purple, yellow, and red outfit billowed around him as he tumbled into his first set of aerial maneuvers.

Joe was the second to exit the airplane. As soon as he cleared the wing, he twisted and turned, using aerodynamic changes in his posture to execute a variety of acrobatics. Out of the corner of his eye, he observed Antonio, still flipping and flopping like a falling peacock.

6 Terrence Drops a Load

Joe twisted his body to get a look at Terrence, who had just jumped. Terrence was in trouble. His chute was gone—the whole chute. He was holding out the silk of his skydiving outfit to add a bit of resistance, but it wouldn't be enough to keep him from reaching terminal velocity and being crushed on the ground below.

I need to time this just right to save him, Joe thought. And me without a calculator.

He turned his back to his falling friend and faced the ground. He gripped his ripcord and pulled. A colorful flow of silk billowed out from his pack, catching the wind and slowing Joe's descent. When the parachute was fully deployed, Joe's downward momentum was momentarily reversed. The shift in velocity brought him close to Terrence.

"Need a lift?" Joe joked, even though he knew his friend could not hear him.

Joe grabbed Terrence around the waist, and the stuntman wrapped his arms around Joe's chest. The two gave each other weak smiles.

Terrence cocked his head to the side and pointed, indicating a bull's-eye target painted on the field of grass below them.

Might as well land with flair, Joe mused. He worked the cords of the parachute, mindful to compensate for the extra weight he was carrying. Several minutes later, Joe put both himself and his package down in the center of the bull's-eye.

Their parents met them at the drop zone.

"What happened up there?" Laura Hardy shouted as Brian McCauley began to help Joe out of his chute pack.

Terrence removed his helmet. "As soon as I went into my first tumble, my pack just tore away from my body." Terrence hugged his father, and then he tried to hug Joe but couldn't, because Laura Hardy was there before him.

"Thanks for the save, man."

"That's what I'm here for, T."

"Was the pack buckled properly?" Mr. Hardy asked.

"Snapped it on myself," Terrence replied.

"Could it have had a faulty strap?" Joe asked.

"Or a cut one," Brian McCauley offered.

"I'd like to take a look at the pack," Mr. Hardy said.

"Good luck finding it," Joe stated flatly. "It could have fallen just about anywhere."

"Well, as far as I'm concerned, this competition is over for you, son," Brian McCauley said.

"Not by a long shot," Terrence said, refusing his dad's advice. "It was bad luck, that's all."

"I'm serious," Brian said.

"So am I, Dad. I'm finishing what I started."

Before the senior McCauley could argue further, Antonio Lawrence came strutting up.

"Didn't you boys know this was a singles competition?" he joked. "What's the matter, Terrence? Can't 'air dance' on your own?"

"Shut up," Terrence spat at Antonio. "I lost my parachute. While you were air dancing, Joe was busy being a hero."

"Oh," Antonio mocked, "a hero. Hey, you can blame your equipment if you want. It'll give you something to cry about when I run away with the prize."

Terrence lost his cool and lunged at Antonio. Mr. Hardy and Brian grabbed him before he could attack his rival.

Joe stepped between Antonio and Terrence. "Listen, wise guy," he said. "This is far from over. And before it's done, the only prize you'll walk away with is egg on your face, if not a whole mess of trouble on the side."

Antonio stared at Joe. Then he cracked a wide smile. "Whatever you say, little hero," he said, and turned to walk away.

Daredevil Fest was delayed for an hour while the competition's organizers discussed the skydiving "accident." At Terrence's insistence, however, and with no evidence that the problem with the parachute pack was anything more than faulty equipment, Daredevil Fest resumed.

The other competitors prepared for the skydiving competition, while Joe and Terrence ate a light brunch. The two competitors were joined by Frank. Fenton and Laura Hardy and Brian McCauley decided to go watch the remaining skydivers.

"I hope you had better luck than we did," Joe said to his brother.

"Compared to you," Frank replied, "I had the easy job."

"So what did you find out?" Terrence asked.

"I hacked into the Department of Motor Vehicles' database. The license plate number for the truck that almost sent us over the cliff is registered to a company—Silver Lining Productions. Ring any bells?"

"Bells?" Joe said excitedly. "It sets off a whole fireworks display."

"How so?" Frank asked.

"I had a little run-in with Phil Silver, owner of Silver Lining Productions," Joe said. "He had 'suspect' written all over him."

Joe went on to explain his earlier encounter with the slick businessman.

"So he left you with the impression that he could be trying to harm Terrence?" Frank asked.

"I don't think he'd want to kill me," Terrence said.

"Maybe not kill you," Joe said. "But he might be trying to put a scare into you so you'll leave stunt work and sign with him."

"Well, I'd say his scares are pretty risky," Frank said. "An M-80 at home and a bomb in a trailer are definitely enough to kill Terrence and a whole crowd."

"He might have an if-I-can't-have-him-nobody-will attitude," Joe offered.

"Could be," Frank conceded. "Although it's a little sick. In any case, he definitely bears a closer look, and I'm going to head over to his offices now."

"Great," Joe said.

"Yeah," Terrence agreed. "Joe and I have to get to our next event."

The next event was a hang glider race. Joe and Terrence rode in a van with Caleb and a couple of the event coordinators up to Aceto-Zimmer Bluff, where the race would begin.

"The bluff is an awesome place for a race," Caleb said. "Have you ever glided there, T?"

"Yeah, I filmed a stunt for the movie *Rhonda and Roseanne* there."

"You did the car-off-the-cliff stunt?" Joe asked. "I loved that movie. Hey, that was a Michael Shannon flick, right?"

"Yeah," Terrence said. "When he was younger."

"And could act at least a little," Caleb added.

The three young men laughed. Joe was getting to like Caleb.

"So fill me in on Aceto-Zimmer Bluff," Joe said.

Caleb unfolded a detailed map of the area. He showed Joe the high oceanside cliff that would mark the start of the race. He traced his finger along the route.

"There are pylons along the beach," Caleb said, "that anchor helium balloons. Those are your markers. You need to fly around the first two markers and then make a sharp turn toward this cove."

"Be careful at the cove," Terrence warned. "The updrafts there are treacherous."

"Believe it, Little Joe," Caleb added. "You'll dive through the cove and fly under a rock outcropping that sort of looks like a bridge. Hit that spot with too much air under your wings and you'll be cliff-pizza on the huge rocks below."

Joe examined the map, locking the stunt flyers' advice in his mind. He noted where all the turn markers were, three on the beach and one off-shore. He didn't think he could win the race, but he certainly wanted to be in the competition.

When the van arrived at Aceto-Zimmer Bluff, Joe and Terrence took some time to examine their hang gliders. After the parachute incident, Joe wanted to be sure that the hang gliders had not been touched.

Satisfied that the equipment was not sabotaged, Joe and Terrence mounted their hang gliders.

The two were matched against each other in the second qualifying heat. Caleb and Antonio had just completed their race, and though the conceited Lawrence had just barely edged out the fun-loving stuntman, both competitors posted very impressive times. Joe and Terrence would be hard-pressed to fly fast enough to qualify for the next round.

"Good luck, Joe," Terrence said.

"I'm here to watch your back," Joe replied, "but I'll give you a run for your money."

The race began. Terrence vaulted into the air, and used his superior skill to gain an early lead. Aceto-Zimmer Bluff dropped away behind them, and the two flyers dove toward the first set of beach markers. Joe had a bit of trouble making the sharp turn toward the cove, so he lost sight of Terrence for a moment.

Joe tightened his legs to streamline his profile a bit more as he entered the cove. He glanced down at the rocks below him. The ocean waves crashed against the rocks, splashing water high into the air. Joe jigged his body to the side to keep the water from glancing off his wings.

Joe avoided the sea spray, but raising the glider

allowed too much air to get under his wings. He exited the cove on an updraft that propelled him at a steep angle. He had too much altitude and knew that he wouldn't be able to make the sharp turn around the marker fifty yards down the beach from the rocky cove. Still, he headed toward the marker to finish the race even if he wouldn't post a good time.

As Joe angled toward the marker, he spotted Terrence a dozen yards ahead and below him. The seasoned stunt flyer had already made the turn and would quickly head out toward the ocean for the final turn marker. Joe admired how Terrence handled his glider, floating effortlessly just above the treacherous rock outcroppings.

Suddenly something else came into Joe's field of vision. It was small and moving fast, and it was coming up from behind Terrence. At first Joe couldn't make out what the object was, but he was certain where it was aimed.

Then Joe realized that the object was a remote-controlled model airplane. He felt helpless as he watched the plane fly straight through the wing of Terrence's hang glider, ripping the fabric. The wing collapsed, and Terrence went plummeting toward the jagged rocks below.

7 Cut and Run

Joe twisted his body. Thanks to his accidental altitude gain, he had a chance of saving his friend.

A chance, he thought, but only one.

Joe pointed the nose of his hang glider down, and the craft immediately began to lose altitude. As it descended, the hang glider gained speed, closing the gap between Joe and Terrence.

The stuntman struggled to keep his own craft together. The hole in the wing forced Terrence to let go of the guide bar so that he could stretch out his arms to bolster both wings.

To Joe, Terrence looked like a wounded bird. With his arms spread out as they were, Terrence could not steer his craft. The hang glider went into a slow spin as it lost altitude. Joe broke into a sweat. He was gaining on Terrence but not fast enough.

He'll hit the rocks, Joe thought. I have to knock him clear.

Joe was still slightly above and a few yards away from Terrence. He knew that in just a few moments Terrence would smash into the rocks in the shallow water below.

"I hope the water's warm," Joe said out loud. He let go of his guide bar. Doing so caused Joe's feet to swing forward with a violent jerk. As his body's momentum shifted, he grabbed hold of the emergency strap release on his harness. He pulled the release, and his body began to fall away from his glider.

As soon as his feet were clear of the glider, Joe pulled his knees up to his chest. He arched his back as his legs came up, thus putting his body into a sort of backward somersault.

He rotated twice, and as he came out of the second revolution, Joe kicked his legs away from his body.

"Contact!" Joe shouted, hoping that he had calculated the maneuver correctly. His feet flailed outward, smashing into the side of Terrence's collapsed hang glider.

The force of the blow had the desired effect. Terrence was violently pushed a few yards to the side. He hit the water, missing the jagged rocks by no more than four feet. Joe's own momentum splashed him into the water nearly on top of Terrence. Buoyed by the fabric of Terrence's demolished hang glider, the two young men floated in the Pacific Ocean.

"You—?" Joe struggled to gain his breath.

Terrence nodded his head, indicating that he was okay. Joe smiled.

Three minutes later a Daredevil Fest safety crew motored up to the two exhausted competitors. Veteran stuntwoman Donna Roman, along with lifeguard Justin Stanfield, fished Terrence and Joe out of the bobbing waves.

"Oxygen?" Stanfield offered a mask to Terrence and Joe, who were both having a little trouble catching their breath. Both took a long drag from the oxygen tank.

"What happened out there?" Donna asked.

"You wouldn't believe me if I told you," Terrence replied.

Both Roman and Stanfield gave Terrence a quizzical look.

"Equipment failure," Joe stated flatly as he watched the remains of Terrence's hang glider sink beneath the surface of the water. He glanced at Terrence to indicate that no more information than that should be shared with the rescue team.

"That's twice now," Donna commented as she put the boat into gear.

"You've got a dark cloud over you," Stanfield added as he draped warm blankets around both wet young men.

Joe and Terrence just nodded.

Twenty minutes later, as Terrence and Joe changed into dry clothes, their parents came bursting into the competitors' trailer.

"What was it this time?" Brian McCauley asked. "Sniper?"

"Low-flying aircraft," Terrence said.

"What?" Mr. Hardy asked.

"It was one of those remote-controlled model airplanes," Joe explained. "It came swooping in on T and cut straight through his wing."

"Did you see what direction it came from?" Mr. Hardy asked.

"It came from the direction of Aceto-Zimmer Bluff," Joe said. "And then it spiraled into the ocean after shredding the wing of the hang glider."

"Well, that finishes it," Brian said. "Someone's definitely trying to knock you out of this competition—if not permanently—and I say we give him what he wants."

"Dad!" Terrence protested.

"Mr. McCauley," Joe cut in, "if we take T out of visible circulation, we may lose our best opportunity to flush his attacker into the open."

"But that means my son is nothing but bait," Brian said.

"Joe's right," Mr. Hardy offered. "Whoever is behind this appears to be willing to come after Terrence wherever he is or whatever he's doing. I'm not keen on exposing T to any danger, but Daredevil Fest may be our best forum to trip up this villain."

"But that puts a bull's-eye on my son's chest."

"It is my chest, Dad," Terrence said. "And we McCauleys don't live in fear."

"All right, we can see where this is heading," Mr. Hardy said. "Let's just let Terrence stay in the games. And the assignments stay the same. Joe, you make that target on Terrence's chest harder to hit. Meanwhile, Brian and I are going to hunt up some scuba equipment. I want to do a little late-night Pacific Ocean diving to see if we can recover that model plane. That could be a good clue."

* * *

74

While Joe and Terrence had been gliding above the ocean, Frank was doing some legwork on the ground. Knowing that the truck that played bumper cars with them the other night was registered to Silver Lining Productions, Frank drove over to their offices.

Seeing the building, Frank got the distinct impression that Phil Silver was a very conservative and shrewd businessman. His office was one of a few in a small Santa Monica four-story office building. Unlike most people who try to set themselves up as Hollywood high rollers, Silver had spent his money wisely. Modest office, probably a lean staff, and as his DMV search had revealed, only one company truck and one company car.

Being a smart money manager didn't put him above attempted murder though, Frank thought. He scanned the parking lot for the truck. If he could find the vehicle with any damage on it, it could be key evidence.

There were very few cars in the lot on a Saturday afternoon, and the pickup truck was not among them.

He probably took it to a body shop to cover himself, Frank thought.

Frank made his way into the building. Inside the lobby, there was a cleaning woman sweeping the floor and a little boy, probably her son, playing with action figures. Neither one so much as glanced up at Frank.

Frank scanned the directory and saw that the complex held only seven businesses. Silver Lining shared the second floor with the law offices of Drake & Zaccheo.

"Well, if he's guilty," Frank mused, "Silver won't have far to travel to get legal counsel."

Frank made his way across the lobby to the stairwell. He walked up to the second floor. After making sure the hallway was empty, Frank left the stairwell. The door to Drake & Zaccheo was closed.

He made his way down the hall to Silver Lining Productions. The office door was closed and locked, but there was no indication of any sophisticated security system.

Low rent probably means low security, Frank thought. He took out his lockpick set and examined the two locks on the Silver Lining door. He selected one small and one oversize pick and within a matter of seconds was inside the office.

Frank was right about Silver's business savvy— the man had a spartan office. The reception area had a few chairs for waiting visitors and a desk for a secretary. The workstation was kept neat, Frank noticed.

What I want is probably through there, Frank thought as he quietly closed the main door behind him. He headed for the door to an inner office. Once inside the office, Frank scanned for places to begin his search.

I'll start with the filing cabinet, he thought.

The first two drawers of the cabinet offered little to tie Phil Silver to any attempts on Terrence's life. There were several movie scripts with notes written in the margins. The only indication that Silver even had an interest in Terrence was a penciled reference on one script that it might make a good first film if the stuntman decided to turn actor with Silver Lining.

The third file drawer also bore little fruit. There were lists of contact names—scriptwriters, production crews, agents—but little else.

Frank turned his attention to Silver's desk. He turned on the computer and began to go through the desk drawers while he waited for the machine to boot up.

"Pay dirt," Frank said triumphantly. On top of some papers inside Phil Silver's drawer, there was a third-party life insurance policy quote. The quote was for a $1 million–dollar accidental death policy, and the name of the potential insuree was none other than Terrence McCauley.

Frank began to flip through the insurance paperwork, looking for the beneficiary and any official signatures. Just then, however, a telephone ring broke his concentration.

Frank stared at the phone. After two rings, the answering machine picked up. The volume was turned up rather loud, and Frank was forced to listen to Silver's businesslike greeting.

After the tone, Frank was riveted to the voice that left Phil Silver a message.

"Mr. Silver," came the recognizable voice, "Ian Edrich here. I have something I think you'd be interested in seeing. I'm going to ring your mobile phone, but just in case I don't catch you, call me back as soon as you can. I won't sit on this for long."

"That's an interesting message," came a voice from behind Frank. "But not as interesting as finding you here."

8 Strange Partners

"So," the stranger asked Frank, "who are you and what are you doing here?"

For a split second Frank thought about trying to bluff the stranger who had surprised him in Phil Silver's office, but instead he decided to be evasive.

"I should be asking you that question," Frank said boldly. "What are you doing in Phil Silver's office on a Saturday?"

"Well, seeing as I am Phil Silver," the man replied, "I can come to my office whenever I want."

"Phil Silver, huh," Frank said. "Prove it."

The man held up a set of keys.

"I have the keys," he said. "I didn't have to break in."

Frank knew he could no longer bluff or be evasive. He was caught red-handed, but he still had one trick left—direct confrontation.

"Well, Mr. Silver—if that's who you really are—then you have a lot to answer for."

"Answer for? To some teenager who obviously broke into my office?"

Frank kept his cool. "I'm part of a team hired to investigate the recent attempts on Terrence McCauley's life," Frank said. "And I have to say, you're looking pretty good as a suspect."

"If I'm a murderer," Silver replied, "you just took a big chance being caught alone with me in my office."

"Who said I'm alone?" Frank asked. "I said I'm part of a team. Expect my backup to be close by."

"Don't worry," Silver responded. "You have nothing to fear from me. If you're really here to protect Terrence McCauley, then you can expect full cooperation from me."

"Really?" Frank was surprised. "Given the evidence against you, I would think you'd be bolting for the exit."

"What evidence?"

"Well, let's start with the truck registered to Silver Lining Productions," Frank began, "the truck that tried to run Terrence McCauley off the road the night of the *Flame Broiled* party."

"How do you know it was my truck?"

"I'm pretty good with license plates," Frank replied.

"Did you get a look at the driver?"

"Can't say that I did. The windows are tinted, as you know. But I'm sure once I put my hands on the truck, I'll have all the evidence I need to prove you tried to run us off the road."

"It wasn't me, uh—what is your name?"

"Frank."

"It wasn't me, Frank," Silver began again. "The truck was stolen. I filed a police report Friday morning."

"But the 'accident' happened Thursday night," Frank stated. "So a Friday morning police report gives you plenty of time to ditch the truck."

"I didn't know the truck was missing until I got to work Friday morning," Silver explained. "And, anyway, I have witnesses who can verify that I was elsewhere Thursday night. Check it out if it makes you feel better."

"Oh, I'll check it out," Frank said. "You can be sure of that."

"Look, Frank," Silver said, "I'm not trying to hurt Terrence. In fact, if you ask him, I've been trying to get him to quit stunt work and become an actor for me."

"Maybe you are," Frank responded. "But he has refused to sign with you, so maybe you're looking for revenge."

"Revenge isn't my game," Silver said.

"But maybe insurance scams are," Frank accused. He held up the million-dollar life insurance quote he had found on the desk.

"Good try," Silver said. "But that piece of paper proves nothing."

"Then why have you been looking into accidental death policies on Terrence McCauley?"

"I'm a businessman trying to launch a movie studio. I want Terrence to sign a long-term contract with me as a way to entice investors. That means that people want to know that their investments are protected. Given that Terrence might want to do his own stunts in Silver Lining films, it makes sense for me to see how much it would cost to insure him. If you dig deeper into my desk, you'll find policy quotes on half a dozen people."

"That still doesn't make you any less a suspect,"

Frank said. "You might be looking to get Terrence insured, kill him, and collect."

"Look at the policy you're holding. It's unsigned and is only in effect if Terrence is under contract with Silver Lining. If money was my goal, I wouldn't be trying to hurt him before he was on my payroll."

Frank flipped the pages of the policy. After a moment, he spoke again.

"Okay," he said, "I think you're on the level. But I do have one more question."

"If it'll help keep Terrence safe, you can ask me anything."

"What was that message from Ian Edrich all about? The one I was listening to when you came in."

"That Edrich is some character," Silver said. "He keeps telling me he's going to be the next kingmaker here in Hollywood. Says the press can make or break anybody. He keeps offering me dirt on actors, but I keep turning him down."

"Why?" Frank asked.

"Why does he offer it? Because he's trying to position himself as a man of importance."

"No," Frank said. "I meant, why have you turned him down?"

"I don't do business the same way the rest of

Hollywood does. Movies are an important part of America's past, and the world's future. Movies can be so much more than moneymakers or status symbols. I'm trying to build a company based on principles here. Buying dirt from a weasel like Ian Edrich will just make me as dirty as the other producers here in Hollywood."

"A man of integrity," Frank said. "The world sure needs more of those."

"Thanks," Silver said. "Now get out of my office and go protect Terrence."

It was late afternoon when Frank returned to the Curtis Hotel. The sun was still visible in the western sky, even through the thick haze of pollution that hung over the Los Angeles basin.

Frank had the valet park the rental car, then made his way up to the hotel suite he shared with Joe and his parents. He was surprised to find everyone in the room, including the McCauleys.

"I didn't figure to see you guys back here yet," Frank said. "Wasn't there supposed to be another event after hang gliding?"

"It was canceled," Joe said. "The whole competition might be shut down."

"What happened?" Frank asked.

84

Terrence and Joe filled Frank in on the details of what occurred over the Pacific Ocean.

"So you're saying that the remote-controlled airplane was timed to hit the wing to make Terrence smash into the rocks," Frank stated. "We've got to be dealing with an expert who can get his hands on some good equipment. The bomb, the plane. What's next?"

"I don't want there to be a next," Brian McCauley interjected.

"None of us do," Mrs. Hardy said comfortingly.

"So what's our next move?" Frank asked.

"Dad's going swimming," Joe replied.

His brother gave him a puzzled look.

"Brian and I are going to do some diving off the cove while we still have some light, to see if we can find the plane. It might yield something."

"What about the rest of us?" Joe asked.

"The rest of you are going to rest, have a good dinner, long showers, and stay safe for one night here at the hotel," Mrs. Hardy said. "No need to put you into any further danger by having you traipse around Hollywood."

"But, Mom—" Joe began to protest.

"Let it go, Joe," Frank said. "I've seen that look in Mom's eyes before. There's no use arguing."

* * *

It wasn't until after ten that Fenton Hardy and Brian McCauley returned to the Curtis Hotel. Their dive had been a success. Mr. Hardy held a damaged model airplane in one hand.

"A model of a jet fighter plane?" Joe was surprised. "I thought most models were of classic aircraft."

"They usually are," Brian said. "But this one is a custom design. It's a pusher model. The propeller is in back. We couldn't find the nose section, but I'm betting it was sharpened to a point to rip through the hang glider fabric."

"Pretty ingenious," Frank said. "How do we find the person who was flying it?"

"Well, Daredevil Fest is closed tomorrow while the officials decide the fate of the contest," Joe said. "We could check out where this plane may have come from."

"Sounds good," Mr. Hardy said.

"But let's not all get caught up in that," Frank suggested. "Even with Phil Silver off the suspect list, there're still plenty of other people to check out."

"So we'll split up," Joe said. "Assignment?"

"I've got a lunch date with Pam Sydney," Mrs. Hardy stated. "I convinced her yesterday that I'd be a good way to get to Terrence."

"Way to go, Mom!" Joe said proudly. "Okay, I'll take Antonio. Any ideas on where to pick up his trail, T?"

"Yeah, there's a church over on Pulaski Road that he goes to on Sundays. He never misses. Even refuses to do stunts before noon on Sundays."

"Great," Frank said. "And I'll set up surveillance on Michael Shannon. We haven't given him much thought since he tried to choke that reporter, Ian Edrich, two nights ago."

"That leaves checking out the hobby shops to Brian, Terrence, and me," Mr. Hardy said. "A rig like this, even a custom-built one, had to get its parts from somewhere."

After getting a good night's sleep, Frank awoke Sunday morning before five. He showered, dressed, and ate a light breakfast before heading off into the Hollywood Hills. Terrence had given him directions to Michael Shannon's home.

Frank arrived just after sunrise and spent a few minutes surveying the area. Shannon's house occupied a corner lot in a very posh neighborhood. A seven-foot-high wall blocked Frank's view of the house. However, Frank discovered that if he climbed a tree at the edge of the woods across the street from the house, he could see into the actor's large backyard. Plus, this particular spot allowed Frank to remain hidden while observing Shannon.

His early morning arrival quickly paid dividends. Only ten minutes after settling into his perch, Frank saw the actor exit the patio door and jump into his swimming pool. Frank became bored, however, watching Shannon swim laps for over thirty minutes.

Well, it's a good way to stay in shape, Frank thought as Shannon finally stepped out of the pool. Frank watched the actor towel off, then saw that something had suddenly drawn the man's attention. Shannon picked up a cordless phone from the poolside table and spoke into it for only a minute.

Frank watched the whole scene, but lost sight of Shannon when he went back into his house.

I've probably seen all his backyard activity today, Frank thought. An early morning call like that might have been a summons to go somewhere.

Playing on his hunch, Frank climbed down from the tree and went to his car. He had parked the car in a spot that gave him a good view of Shannon's front gate.

When the actor left his house, Frank was ready. He followed Michael Shannon's green sports car at a discreet distance.

Frank was led farther up into the Hollywood Hills. Here the homes were farther apart and the woods thicker. Finally, Shannon left the road and turned his car into a forest.

Frank pulled off the road and entered the woods on foot. He used a pair of binoculars to watch the actor, who had parked his car and gotten out.

Frank saw Shannon approach another car, a Jeep. Unfortunately, the bushes and the open door of the vehicle blocked Frank's view of the person with Shannon. Frank could see, however, that the person the actor had met had given him a large manila envelope. Frank watched as the actor pulled what looked like a set of enlarged photographs from the envelope. Frank couldn't make out what the pictures were, but they made Shannon very happy. Frank could see him smile widely as he handed the pictures and envelope back to the other person.

The mystery person got into the Jeep, but Frank still could not see who it was. He made a quick decision: following the Jeep might yield better results than watching Shannon go through his Sunday routine.

Frank raced back to his car and was in position to follow the Jeep when it left the woods. After a forty-five-minute drive, the Jeep finally stopped in front of a low-rent apartment complex. Frank parked across the street.

"Well, I'll be . . ." Frank said to himself as he saw the driver of the Jeep get out of the vehicle.

Without hesitating, Frank jumped out of his car and raced across the street. The person had just entered the door of a first-floor apartment. Before he could close the door, Frank had put his shoulder against the wood and muscled his way into the apartment.

"Sort of strange, don't you think," Frank said gruffly, "that you and Michael Shannon would have a friendly get-together?"

9 Spin City

"Who . . . what?" The person Frank was confronting began to stammer.

Frank was not about to let his suspect regain his composure. "Don't play dumb, Edrich," he said.

Frank could see that the lanky reporter was scared. It must have been the element of surprise, but whatever it was, Frank decided to press his advantage.

"I just saw you with Michael Shannon," Frank said. "You guys must have made up pretty fast, seeing as the last time you were together he tried to choke the life out of you."

"I, he—" Edrich started to say.

Frank kept the heat turned up. "So, are you blackmailing him? I saw you show him some pictures."

The reporter put his hands and the manila envelope behind his back.

"You might as well let me see them," Frank said. "Or I can call the police and you can show what's inside that envelope to them."

"Okay, okay," Edrich said, holding out the envelope to Frank, who took the pictures out. He studied them for a second.

"What's this all about?" Frank asked. "All I see here are a bunch of photos of Michael Shannon in a dark bar with some woman I don't recognize. You really are trying to blackmail him."

"No, it's not that," Edrich replied.

"Out with it," Frank said, "or I call the police."

"We're, well, sort of working together," Edrich stammered.

Frank shook his head in disbelief. "Start explaining," he said.

"Shannon's career is flagging," the reporter began. "He's too clean-cut for today's Hollywood. People today like to see a bad boy up on the screen. It's the day of the antihero, and Michael

Shannon is trying to remold himself. Without a new image, his career is sunk."

"So a couple of fistfights, attacking a reporter, a mystery woman in a seedy club, and he figures he can get a new lease on his career?" Frank asked.

"Exactly. We tarnish his name, sling a little mud on his pearly white image, generate some heat around him, and *boom,* he's headlines again." Edrich smiled at the beauty of his plan.

"Where do you fit in?" Frank was more than curious.

"I know Shannon's cousin," Edrich explained. "I got to Hollywood hoping to make a name for myself as an entertainment reporter. The cousin hooked me up with Shannon, and we concocted this plot to light a fire under both of our careers. Two stars for the price of one."

"Does your plot include trying to kill Terrence McCauley?" Frank asked.

"No," Edrich nearly shouted. "No way. McCauley was only a convenient tool the night of the *Flame Broiled* thing. He was standing there, so Shannon ad-libbed a little. The whole town knows they've never liked each other."

"That's a convenient and unconvincing response," Frank said flatly. "You're going to have to do better than that."

"Look, I'm being straight here," Edrich pleaded. He ran his long skinny fingers through his bleached blond hair.

"Think about it," he continued. "What quicker way to tank an already-sinking career than by being tossed in jail for murder? You can't do much acting from behind bars. Kill McCauley and get caught, and Shannon's doing himself in as well. The guy's only trying to remake his image. He's an actor. The only thing he could kill is a good script. He's not looking to do any harm to that stuntman."

"Makes sense," Frank said. He turned to leave the reporter's apartment.

"Oh," Frank added, turning to face Edrich once more, "don't think I won't let it out what you two are up to if you tell anyone about our talk. Then you'd have to start looking for a new job," Frank added. "I hear they need ghostwriters for kids' books."

While Frank was with Ian Edrich, Joe was across town sitting outside a church on Pulaski Road in the other rental car.

After an hour, with only occasional bursts of music from inside the building to break the monotony of the wait, the service ended. Joe immediately caught sight of Antonio Lawrence. The stuntman exited the church and spent a few minutes talking to some people. After exchanging a few hugs, he got into his blue convertible sports car.

Does everybody here have a nice car? Joe mused. Maybe we should move.

Antonio pulled his car out of the church parking lot and zipped down Pulaski Road. Joe put his car in gear. He lay back a bit and followed just close enough to keep Lawrence in view.

I hope I don't do anything to tip him off, Joe thought as he decelerated a bit and fell even farther back.

Joe saw Lawrence make a sudden, unsignaled turn and guessed he'd been spotted. His guess was confirmed when Antonio made two more unsignaled turns in rapid succession.

Joe tried to close the gap between the two cars, but he couldn't risk speeding or causing an accident.

Now that he knew he was being tailed, Antonio made more sharp turns and played tricks with traffic to try to shake Joe. The younger Hardy hung tough and kept his prey in sight.

When Antonio led Joe out of the downtown area and up into the hills, it gave Joe an opportunity to open up the car a bit. He pressed down on the gas pedal as he watched the blue convertible careen around a bend in the road.

As Joe rounded the same bend, however, his eyes widened in horror. The road narrowed suddenly and Joe watched Antonio pull a maneuver that only a stunt driver could accomplish in such a confined space: the man hit his brakes and whirled the car around one hundred and eighty degrees. He came speeding straight at Joe!

10 Driver's Ed

Joe slammed on the brakes and jerked the wheel to the right, bringing the car to a skidding halt. The rental car was turned sideways, straddling both lanes of the road.

Antonio also slammed on his brakes and turned his wheel. When his blue convertible came to a complete stop, his driver's-side door was less than a foot from the driver's-side door of the rental.

With unbelievable speed, Antonio was out of his car and in Joe's face. The stuntman had left his car door open, which brought it to rest against Joe's door, trapping him inside his car.

"What do you think you're doing?" Antonio

yelled at Joe through the open window. He leaned into the car and grabbed Joe by the shirt collar.

Joe quickly outlined his options. There were none. The way the cars were positioned, he was trapped. The rear of the vehicle was too close to the rocky cliffside wall to use reverse as an escape route. And to drive forward could mean plunging over the cliff if he did it too quickly.

"What am I doing?" Joe questioned. "You're the one who drove down the hill in the wrong lane aimed directly at me."

"I'll ask again. Why are you following me?"

"It's what I do," Joe replied. "I always keep an eye on anyone who might be trying to kill a friend of mine."

Antonio laughed and released his grip on Joe.

"You're funny," he said, and patted Joe's chest once. "I could demolish you at any time, and you just get right in my face. You have guts."

"And brains," Joe said. "Brains enough to know that you'd love to see Terrence go down so you could win Daredevil Fest and be the top stuntman in town."

"Oh, I'll be the top dog in this town," Antonio said with confidence. "And I'd love to see that pretty boy knocked low. But try to hurt him? No way."

"You're just covering up," Joe said.

"Covering up what? When I beat Terrence for the top spot, I don't want him saying it was a tainted victory. If I don't beat him cleanly, then people won't take me seriously."

"But any victory you'd get now will be suspicious," Joe replied. "With two attempts on his life occurring in the first two events, the lead you have now means nothing."

"First of all, there are a lot more events to go, so no lead is safe. And second, those so-called attempts on his life were probably caused by incompetence," Antonio said.

"Of course you'd have to say all this if you were trying to kill him. I don't buy that what's happened to Terrence in the past couple of weeks, especially during the competition, was because of incompetence. And you certainly have motive, opportunity, and expertise to pull all of this off."

"Sure," Antonio answered. "I could pull any of it off. But I'm not."

"Can you prove it?" Joe asked.

"I don't have to. I'm innocent until proven guilty."

"So all I have is your word."

"Yeah," Antonio said, "that's all you have."

"So where does that leave us?" Joe asked.

"It leaves *you,* man," Antonio responded. "You investigate anything you want. Me, I'm going to visit my mother."

Antonio returned to his sports car. Without a backward glance, he put the convertible in gear and sped away.

When Joe returned to the Curtis Hotel, he found a message from Frank to meet at Terrence's house. After a quick shower, Joe got back in the rental car and went to hook up with his brother.

"What's all this?" Joe asked as he entered the McCauleys'. He pointed to two large boxes in the entryway.

"Check it out," Frank said as he led his brother into the den.

"So he's got you hooked?" Joe asked Terrence, nodding at the brand-new computer that sat on an oak desk.

"Welcome to the Information Age." Frank smiled.

"Your brother convinced me that I shouldn't live without one of these," Terrence said. "So he went with me and helped me pick out some equipment."

"I didn't want to go to the library again to do research," Frank admitted.

"So, what are we researching?" Joe asked.

"Depends on what you came up with," Frank stated.

"You first," Joe said. He slumped into a chair.

"Okay," Frank started. "The short version is that I don't think Michael Shannon is the one trying to kill T."

"What brought you to that conclusion?"

"Well, I did find out he was up to something— something to jump-start his career. It turns out that he's trying to cultivate a Hollywood bad boy image. Killing Terrence is not the sort of scandal he'd need to boost his career."

"I took him for all bark anyway," Joe said. "Antonio, on the other hand—that guy might have plenty of bite."

Joe filled Frank and Terrence in on his run-in with the cocky stuntman.

"So, where does that leave us?" Terrence asked.

"Pretty much with nothing," Frank answered. "He could have you in his sights, or he could be telling the truth."

"T," Joe asked, "do you know much about Antonio?"

"Just what he lets people know," Terrence said. "Which is nothing but what's in his bio. That, and the church he likes to go to."

"Maybe we can check out his past, his background," Frank offered.

"How?" Terrence asked.

Frank smiled at the computer.

For the next two hours Frank wielded the machine's keyboard as if it were a sword. He made his way through the World Wide Web, searching for information on Antonio Lawrence. Frank looked into the local records of the various places Antonio had lived, but came up with nothing other than previous addresses, paid parking tickets, and one arrest for disorderly conduct with charges dropped.

"We have nothing more than we did before," Terrence said.

"Research doesn't always yield the results you want," Frank stated.

"You can say that again," Mr. Hardy commented as he entered the den.

"So, the sweep of the hobby stores came up empty?" Joe asked.

"Yeah," Mr. Hardy replied. "There are just too many suppliers and too many buyers of radio-controlled equipment. After talking with some shop owners, we realized that pretty much any skilled hobbyist could have made the modifications to that plane that took out the hang glider."

"But the trip wasn't a total loss," said Brian Mc-Cauley as he entered the den carrying a large red-and-white box. "I see I'm not the only one who did some shopping. Nice computer."

"What do you have there, Dad?"

"A remote-controlled replica of flying champ Scott Pellegrino's Zano 2000."

"A what?" Frank asked.

"A Zano 2000!" Joe was excited.

"The very one flown by Pellegrino when he won the world championship. You like airplane racing, Joe?"

"I love it," Joe responded as he gazed at the pictures on the model's box. "This is one fast, sleek aircraft. First time I saw it in action, I couldn't believe the kind of acceleration and speed a propeller plane could generate."

Just then everyone heard the front door open.

"Where is everybody?" Mrs. Hardy called from the hallway. The men all exited the den and joined her as she made her way to the kitchen.

"Ah, the last of our investigators," Mr. Hardy beamed. "Come up with anything?"

"More than you, from the sound of that question," Laura replied. She sat down at the kitchen table.

"So spill, Mom," Frank said. "Is Pam good for the crime?"

"Most certainly not!" Laura exclaimed. "The only thing that girl is good for is a broken heart. Her own, most likely. She's head over heels in love with Terrence. But she doesn't know how to express herself in any other way than with noise and flash. She loves him—she doesn't want to kill him."

Mrs. Hardy looked at Terrence. "You don't have to date Pam if you don't want to," she said, "but be her friend. There's more to her than you see."

"Unfortunately, that 'more' doesn't get us any closer to who's behind all this," Brian McCauley said.

"So what next?" Joe asked.

Just then the phone rang. Terrence picked it up, and after listening for a few seconds hung up.

"Good news or a threat?" Mr. Hardy asked.

"Great news," Terrence said. "Daredevil Fest is back on for tomorrow!"

The next morning the contestants gathered on the back lot of Mad Alliance Studios. There was a spectators' grandstand set up at one end of the lot. The rest of it was set up as an obstacle course, complete with pylons, small ramps, gates, oil slicks, and speed bumps.

"Wow, that's some course," Joe said to Terrence. "We're driving sports cars?"

"Better than that," Terrence replied. He pointed to a warehouse at the far end of the course. The warehouse doors opened and two eighteen-wheel semi-trucks came rolling out.

"Awesome!" Joe shouted.

The first Daredevil Fest contestant to drive was Antonio. Both trucks were kept idling, but only one was driven at a time. This way the second truck could start immediately while the first truck was being refueled so that each racer would drive a vehicle with the same fuel weight, making race results more accurate.

Antonio made a decent run, but his time was not spectacular. He missed one of the gates and was penalized, opening the door for the other contestants to move up in the standings.

Terrence was up next. He began his run while Joe mounted the semi that Antonio had just used. He watched Terrence start out fabulously. Then he lost sight of the truck as it rounded the warehouse. That part of the course took the semi out of Joe's sight for a minute.

When the truck came into view, it was moving much faster than Antonio had been.

Joe realized in a flash that the truck was moving too fast. Then he heard the semi's airhorn blast. He couldn't make out Terrence's face inside the cab, but from the way the stuntman was laying on the horn, Joe knew that something was wrong. Very wrong, Joe realized, as the truck gained speed and headed straight for the grandstands!

11 Smash-Up Derby

"All right," Joe said out loud. "Now even I want Terrence to quit Daredevil Fest!" Joe squinted so he could bring the stuntman's face into focus.

No steering, Joe guessed, and no brakes.

Terrence's eighteen-wheeler was still on a course headed straight for the grandstand.

"Clear out!" Frank Hardy yelled. He began to scramble off the grandstand, prompting other spectators to leave their seats as well.

"Come on! Move, move, move!" Mr. Hardy yelled, taking up his son's call. The spectators all began to move. Some ran from the grandstands.

Others leaped off the side, not even worrying about the short drop to the ground.

Confident that everyone was clear, Mr. Hardy and Frank ran, just as Terrence's truck smashed through the iron and aluminum structure and veered off away from the grandstand.

Meanwhile, Joe Hardy had thrown his eighteen-wheeler into gear. The semi lurched forward, slowly picking up speed as Joe worked the truck's gears.

As he had done with the hang glider, Joe quickly figured a possible intercept angle from where he was to where he could deflect Terrence's truck. Still, crashing two eighteen-wheel trucks together was not what Joe had in mind.

I need to be more subtle, Joe thought as he swung his truck parallel to Terrence's vehicle.

Joe jerked the wheel and bumped Terrence's truck. He did it again and again, using the gentle nudging to cut the out-of-control semi's speed.

This isn't working fast enough, Joe said to himself. He shot a glance at Terrence, hoping the stuntman had a fresh idea.

Terrence pointed. Joe followed his finger and saw that Terrence was indicating a large concrete building dead ahead.

Well, crashing his truck into the concrete would

stop it, Joe thought. Probably kill T, but it would stop the truck.

"I hope there's a second part to your plan!" Joe shouted even though he knew Terrence couldn't hear him over the roaring engines.

With both trucks traveling over forty miles per hour, Joe violently jerked the wheel of his vehicle and smashed it into the other semi. The jolt was insufficient to alter Terrence's course. He was still angled straight at the building.

Joe knew how desperate Terrence was when he saw him open the driver's-side door of his speed-ing truck and climb out of the cab.

Where is he going? Joe thought in disbelief. Then he caught on to Terrence's plan.

Joe sped up and closed the distance between the two vehicles once more. He maneuvered his truck so that his front end was just short of Ter-rence's driver's-side door as the semis ran parallel to each other.

"Now would be good!" Joe shouted. He wasn't certain that Terrence heard him, but at that pre-cise moment Terrence did propel himself away from his eighteen-wheeler.

The stuntman landed with a thud on the front hood of Joe's truck.

"Hang on!" Joe screamed. He violently jerked

the wheel just in time to veer away from the concrete building. In his sideview mirror, Joe saw the now-empty semi smash into the concrete building. Both the truck and the wall crumpled, but at least the rampaging eighteen-wheeler had come to a complete stop and hadn't burst into flames.

Joe eased his truck to a stop. Terrence smiled at him through the windshield, and Joe smiled back. As they both got to the ground, Frank, Mr. Hardy, and Brian McCauley came jogging up.

"What the Evel Knievel happened out there!" Brian McCauley shouted.

"I'm not sure," Terrence replied. "The run was going great when all of a sudden—*pop*—she jerked up from the ground a bit, like she'd hit something in the road."

"Did you hit something?" Frank asked.

"Not that I saw," Terrence replied. "But I was concentrating on the obstacles, so there could have been something in the road. In any case, after the jolt, I had no steering and no brakes! I couldn't even downshift to cut speed."

"We figured as much," Joe said.

"I want to get a look at the truck," Frank said. The older Hardy brother jogged over to the concrete building that had ended the eighteen-wheeler's joyride.

When he got to the scene, somebody else was already poking around under the vehicle.

"Hey, what are you doing!" Frank asked.

The man, startled by Frank, nearly bumped his head against the bottom of the truck as he stood up. He turned around and glared at Frank. The stranger was tall and painfully thin, and by Frank's guess probably in his midforties. Frank immediately noticed a long thick scar that ran along the man's cheek from his left eye to his jawbone. It was a glaring disfigurement, and Frank tried not to stare.

"I should be asking you that question," the man replied in a deceptively smooth voice. Frank was surprised that such a melodic voice came from such a hard-looking face.

"I came to see what happened," Frank said. "I work with the driver."

"So do I," the man said. "I'm William Thompson, safety consultant for Daredevil Fest."

"Frank Hardy," Frank said. He extended his hand in greeting, but Thompson did not remove either of his own hands from the pockets of the overalls he wore.

"Well, Frank Hardy," he said, "you have no reason to be here, so run along."

With no official reason to remain, Frank simply walked away.

"Who's that William Thompson guy," he asked as he rejoined the group.

"Slim Billy Thompson," Brian McCauley said with a shake of his head. "Now, there's a tragedy."

Frank, Joe, and Mr. Hardy gave the senior McCauley a questioning look, but he just cast his eyes down and stared at the ground deep in thought.

"William 'Slim Billy' Thompson," Terrence said, filling the silence. "He's the safety consultant for this whole event."

"Well, he's not doing all that great a job," Joe stated flatly.

"What's his story?" Frank asked.

"It's a tough one," Terrence began. Before he could say any more, though, he stifled himself.

Slim Billy was approaching. The thin man gave the entire group a steely glare. He obviously had something serious on his mind.

"Terrence," he said tersely as he joined the gathering, "I've got some troubling news."

12 Safety First

"What do you mean, 'troubling news'?" Mr. Hardy asked. "What did you discover?"

"I haven't discovered much of anything yet," Slim Billy replied.

"But . . ." Brian McCauley quizzed.

"But I think enough has happened to warrant a full investigation. I hate to do it, but as safety consultant, I'm hereby shutting Daredevil Fest down."

"What!" Terrence immediately complained. "You can't do that."

"I certainly can," Slim Billy replied calmly in his singsong voice. "And you're the reason why."

"What are you saying?" Joe asked.

"I'm saying that all of these mishaps have happened to Terrence," Slim Billy said. "They could be coincidence, they could be sabotage. . . ."

"Or they could be his incompetence," Antonio said as he joined the gathering.

"You wish!" Terrence shot back at his competition.

"Look," Antonio said, "you're the only one who can't get it together. No reason for all of the competitors to suffer because of you."

"I thought you wanted to win this tournament with Terrence in it," Joe said.

"Sure, I'd like to," Antonio answered. "And I know I can. But I don't want to see the whole thing go down the drain just because T here has lost his edge."

Terrence pressed his angry face into Antonio's. The two were nearly touching noses.

"I have my edge, boy," Terrence said, steamed. "Edge enough to take you down."

Brian McCauley pushed his body between the two hotheads.

"Enough!" he shouted. "This is about more than Daredevil Fest. Somebody wants my son dead, and this has gone way past any game."

"Well, I don't know if anybody is trying to kill

your boy," Thompson said. "But if that is the case, my investigation will uncover any sabotage."

"Can't you investigate while the competition continues?" Terrence asked. He eased a few inches away from Antonio.

"No, and that's final," Slim Billy replied. "I'm concerned for your safety, Terrence," he stated. "Frankly, I'm concerned for all of the competitors' safety."

"Aw, man, this is bogus," Antonio spat out as he flung his hands above his head. He walked away in a huff.

"Well, we appreciate your concern," Joe said. "It's getting tiring, hauling T out of danger. Just please let us know what you find." Joe held out his hand in a gesture of friendship to Slim Billy. The haggard-looking safety consultant absentmindedly took Joe's hand and gave it a weak, very abrupt shake.

Joe immediately noticed that Slim Billy's grip was very strange. Then Joe realized it not only felt weird but oddly familiar. Joe was certain he had encountered the man—or at least his hand—in the past few days.

The skydiving airplane, Joe realized, when the pilot grabbed my shoulder.

Perhaps a bit too obviously, he looked at the

man's right hand as Billy pulled it away and jammed it in his pocket.

"Uh, well," Joe stammered, "I guess we should go get cleaned up."

"Good idea," Brian said. "Thanks again, Billy."

"No problem," Thompson replied. He turned and walked back toward the wrecked eighteen-wheeler. Frank noted that Slim Billy had a serious limp. His left leg was extremely stiff.

"I guess we'll head on back to the house," Mr. Hardy said. "You coming, Frank?"

"Nah, I'm going to stick with Joe and T. We'll see you back there."

Brian and Mr. Hardy said goodbye and left for home.

"Let's hit the trailer and change," Terrence suggested. The three young men began to walk.

"Spill it," Frank said to Joe. "I saw something on your face while you were talking to William Thompson."

"His hand, man. Didn't you notice it?"

"What about it?" Frank asked.

"He has only two fingers and a thumb on his right hand," Joe said. "His middle finger and his pinky are missing. I wonder how he could fly a plane with such a damaged hand."

"What do you mean, 'fly a plane'?" Terrence asked.

"I recognized his strange grip," Joe responded. "He was the one who helped me get into the airplane when we went skydiving."

"So?" Terrence said. "He's the safety coordinator for this show. Plus, he's actually a great pilot. It's not odd that he would pilot the skydiving event."

The three entered the changing trailer. No other competitors were in there, so they had privacy.

"There are no restrictions given his handicap?" Frank asked.

"I'd fly with him," Terrence said.

"You seem to have a lot of respect for the guy," Joe said. He took off his sweaty shirt.

"I guess I do," Terrence said. He got himself a bottle of water from the refrigerator. "He was a great stuntman in his day. He could have been the best."

"I hear a *but* in your voice," Frank said.

"But," Terrence continued, "he was very reckless. He was a big risk taker when he did a stunt. Always pushing the envelope. Studio execs had a love-hate relationship with Slim Billy. He always delivered the most action-packed stunts, but he was a killer on their insurance premiums. Studio accountants used to joke that they needed to take out a 'Slim Billy rider' on the insurance policies if he was working the film."

"So one of his stunts finally caught up with him," Joe said as he put on some fresh shorts.

"I'll say," Terrence said. "I was there when it happened." He slumped down to the couch, obviously depressed by the story he was about to relate.

"It was two years ago," Terrence began. "On the set of *The Bridges of Rodriguez Ridge.*"

"The World War II movie?" Frank asked.

Terrence nodded and continued.

"Anyway, by that time, it was difficult to get other stuntmen to work with Thompson. He was too reckless. But the studio needed a blockbuster, so they went with him as the lead stuntman. I was young and wanted work, so I signed on as well."

Terrence took a drink and stared at the floor.

"We were doing a stunt on a mountainside," he finally said. "There were a lot of explosions as we charged up what was something like a twenty-percent grade. *Boom, bam, bang!* Explosives were detonating all around us. I was in the lead. Then, *boom,* a charge goes off close to me and I lose my footing. Some rocks start to slide. One bounces and hits Slim Billy square . . ."

Terrence choked on his words.

"Hit him square . . ." he started again, but could not proceed.

Frank sat down next to the emotional stunt-man. He put a reassuring hand on his leg.

Terrence never stopped staring at the floor.

"The rock hit him right in the face," Terrence said. Frank and Joe could see that there were tears welling up in their friend's eyes. "Slim Billy fell backward, right onto one of the buried explosive charges just as it detonated. He took shrapnel in his leg and face. It blew off the two fingers from his right hand."

The room fell silent for a minute.

"It wasn't your fault," Joe said reassuringly.

"Actually, that's what the investigation revealed," Terrence replied. "Turns out that there were twice as many charges planted on that hill as there should have been. It was never discovered who planted the extra explosives, but the prevailing theory was that Thompson had done it himself. All in the name of realism. For a better stunt, the man almost killed us both."

Terrence got up from the couch and finished changing into fresh clothes.

"Still," he said, "I can't help feeling I was responsible. Even though Slim Billy has gone out of his way to show that he knows it wasn't my fault."

"Maybe that's why he called off Daredevil Fest," Joe said as they left the trailer. "He probably doesn't want any tragedies happening to the people he feels responsible for."

"You're probably right," Terrence said. "He could never work as a stuntman again after the accident, but he stayed in the business as a coordinator and consultant. In fact, movies he works on these days have the best safety rating in the industry."

Frank looked at the sun as it crawled across the western sky.

"Let's catch an early dinner before heading to your house," he said.

Ninety minutes later the three friends arrived at the McCauley home.

"Looks like everybody's here," Terrence said as they pulled up in front of the house. He pointed at the rental car and his father's truck. The three young men had the other rental car at their disposal while Terrence's beloved sports car was being repaired.

When they got into the house, however, there was nobody there.

"That's odd," Frank said. "Where are the parental units?"

"Beats me," Terrence said.

"Uh, T," Joe said, "did you buy a new tape player when we weren't looking?"

"No," Terrence replied. "Why?"

Joe pointed to a small tape recorder on the living room coffee table.

"I've never seen that before," Terrence said.

All three cautiously approached the tape player. Taped to the front of the device was a note: Let's play.

13 Where Have All the Parents Gone?

" 'Let's play'?" Terrence said. He reached for the Play button on the unfamiliar tape machine. "Maybe my dad's come up with a new way to make sure I don't miss his messages."

"No! Wait!" Frank screamed. He quickly slapped Terrence's hand away from the tape machine.

"What was that for?" Terrence asked, rubbing his wrist.

"It could be booby-trapped," Frank said. "We have no idea who put that machine here. I'd say with all that's gone on lately, it's better to err on the side of caution."

Terrence nodded his head in agreement.

"I'll go check out the rest of the house," Joe said. He headed up the stairs.

Frank crouched down beside the coffee table to get a closer look at the machine.

He scanned the device from every angle without actually touching it.

"I don't see anything unusual," he said softly. He then reached into his back pocket and took out his lockpick set. He chose the longest tool in the kit. With the pick, he gently prodded the machine, moving it ever so gently.

"So far so good," Terrence said, relieved that nothing had exploded.

Frank gently picked up the tape player. He turned it over and examined the battery compartment.

"Four double As," he said. "No special wires or signs that the machine has been modified."

"I guess we should press Play, then," Joe said as he returned to the living room. "The house is clear. No sign of any forced entry."

"Okay, here goes," Frank said. He put the machine back down and pressed Play.

An electronically disguised voice emanated from the machine's tiny speaker.

"No more games," the voice said. "I've given

Terrence a fighting chance to stay alive, but even so, he should be dead by now. And he would be if it wasn't for the meddling Hardy brothers. You two kids think you're so good at this? Let's see how you do with a real challenge. By now you know that your parents aren't around. That's because I have them. I wonder if you two can save their lives and still keep me from killing Terrence. You'll get further instructions by phone at nine P.M. Standard kidnapping rules apply: alert the police and I'll kill my hostages."

The tape machine went silent. Frank pressed the Off button.

"No options," Joe said flatly.

"Not so," Frank interjected. "We may not be able to pick up anything from the voice on the tape. It could have been male or female for all we know, but we still have some suspects we can check out."

"What suspects?" Terrence asked. "Everybody you've checked out on this case has an excuse why it isn't them."

"Then we start by checking out everybody again," Frank stated.

"No time," Joe said. "We could call around to each of our suspects, but if we call the actual culprit, he or she might panic and harm our folks."

"Well, what do we do?" Terrence asked.

"We go with our gut and check out our prime suspect in person."

"Who would be?" Frank asked.

"I'm voting on Antonio Lawrence," Joe said. "I don't like the guy, and I don't trust him."

"If that's your best guess," Frank said, "let's go for it."

"I'll let you know what I find," Joe said, heading for the door.

"No, I'll let you know," Frank said, cutting off his brother. "You and Antonio don't like each other even a little bit. You won't get anything out of him if there's a confrontation."

Joe had to agree with his brother's logic. It was decided that Frank would check out their prime suspect, and Joe would keep a watch on Terrence to make sure the kidnapper didn't try a double-cross by coming back to the house instead of phoning.

As the hour approached nine Joe began to get worried. "Frank should have been back by now," he said. "I hope he hasn't run into any trouble."

"Maybe we should go to Antonio's," Terrence stated.

Just then the telephone rang.

"I guess we'll know something now anyway," Joe

125

said. He reached for the phone and hit the speaker button so both of them could hear the instructions.

"Glad to see you can follow instructions," came the disguised voice through the telephone's speaker. "I want the three of you to drive into the hills. There's a cliff exactly three and seven-tenths miles farther up the hill from where we played bumper cars last week. It's secluded, so we won't get interrupted as this all plays out. And don't take any side trips getting up here. My patience is wearing thin."

The line went dead.

"Well, I get the feeling that our bad guy doesn't know that Frank isn't here," Joe said. "I don't know if that's good news or bad news." Joe picked up a pen from the coffee table and scribbled his brother a note.

"In any case," he said as he wrote, "we can't wait for him to return. We'll have to do this with just the two of us."

"I'm up for it," Terrence said. "Let me gather some stuff from my room. You go get some rope, flashlights, and whatever else you think we might need from the basement."

"Good thinking," Joe said. He stood up and headed for the basement. "We'll make a detective out of you yet," he called.

Joe opened the door to the basement and flicked on the light switch. He was only halfway down the stairs when he heard the door slam shut behind him. The distinctive sound of a deadbolt lock being thrown filled the musty silence.

"What's going on!" Joe shouted as he ran back up the stairs.

He grabbed the door handle and gave it a twist.

"Locked!" he grunted. Joe banged on the door.

"Terrence!" he shouted. "Terrence, let me out of here."

"Sorry, Joe," came the stuntman's voice from the other side of the door. "No can do."

Joe banged on the door again.

"What are you up to, Terrence?" he asked.

"I can't put you in any more danger," Terrence replied. "I have to finish this myself."

"Come on, T. This is no time to go solo on me."

Joe's shout was greeted by silence.

"I'm pleading with you here," Joe continued. "Don't do anything foolish."

Again, only silence.

"T?" Joe yelled. "Oh, man," Joe said. He slumped to sit on the top stair. "He's gonna get himself and our parents killed."

14 All Locked Up
with Someplace
to Go

Forty minutes before Joe found himself locked in the McCauleys' basement, Frank arrived at Antonio Lawrence's home. He parked his car down the block from the house and quietly approached the building on foot.

Frank used a row of hedges that divided Antonio's lawn from that of the neighbors to hide his approach. Certain that he could not be seen by anybody who might be inside Antonio's place, Frank made his way on all fours to a large bush just outside Antonio's living room window. He cautiously peeked through the window. The lights were off, and with the sun now beyond the western horizon, Frank was left with little illumination.

Just then Frank was grabbed from behind. A set of powerful arms had him in a full nelson, and Frank was pulled to his feet.

"What . . . uh . . . ow," Frank grunted as he struggled with his unknown assailant. Frank felt his head being pushed into his chest by the force of the wrestling hold. With practiced smoothness, the older Hardy brother shifted his weight, moved his hip into the body of his attacker, and flipped the man over his shoulder and down to the ground.

Whoever Frank's attacker was, the person was a very skilled fighter. Before Frank could focus his eyes to see his assailant, the figure on the ground kicked out with both legs and tripped Frank. A powerful punch then struck Frank on the back.

Sensing another blow was on its way, Frank rolled away from his attacker and sprang to his feet. His opponent also sprang to his feet and threw a punch straight at Frank's face. Just then Frank made out who his attacker was.

"Enough!" Frank shouted, and blocked the incoming punch. With one fluid motion, Frank turned the block into a wristlock. He twisted, applying enough pressure to force his attacker to his knees.

"I have the advantage now, Antonio," Frank huffed tiredly.

"Hardy?" Uncertainty echoed in Antonio's voice.

"Yeah," Frank replied. "Wait, you didn't know it was me when you grabbed me?" Frank eased the pressure on the stuntman's wrist enough so he could get to his feet.

"No," Antonio replied. "I was stretching after my evening run, and I saw somebody snooping around my house. With all the weird stuff that's been going down lately, I thought maybe somebody was after me."

"You mean, you saw me and thought it was somebody out to get you? I came here thinking you were the one who was trying to harm Terrence."

"For the last time, I am not trying to kill Terrence. Yeah, I want to be top stuntman, but not enough to hurt somebody. That's why I attacked you. I'm beginning to think somebody hates all stuntmen, and I may be the next target."

Frank released his hold on Antonio's wrist.

"Man, that leaves us at square one," Frank said.

"What do you mean?"

"I mean," Frank said, "that now we have no idea who's after Terrence. I can assure you that you are not a target. Whoever wants T dead is definitely doing it for personal reasons."

"Well, I hope you find the guy," Antonio offered. "I may not like the dude, but with Terrence around, I know I always have to be on top of my game."

Antonio held out his hand to Frank. "Just do me a favor," he said. "Terrence is competition enough for me. When this is done, could you and your brother move back to wherever it is you came from? With the way you fight and your brother drives, you'd probably have me and T both flipping burgers while you two carve up all the stunt work."

Frank shook Antonio's hand. "Don't worry," he said. "Joe and I would probably find stunt work too tame compared to what we usually go through, but thanks for the good word."

Frank turned to leave.

"Good luck," Antonio called. "I hope you take this villain down."

It was just after nine when Frank returned to the McCauley house. The first thing he noticed was that Brian McCauley's truck was gone.

Joe and Terrence must have already gotten the call and left, he realized. Frank ran into the house, hoping they'd left a note.

Immediately Frank's attention was grabbed by the sound of his brother's shouting.

"Hello! Frank! Is that you?" came Joe's voice.

"Joe?" Frank shouted. He followed Joe's voice to the basement door and unlocked it. Joe came shooting into the kitchen.

"What's going on?" Frank asked.

"We got the call," Joe replied. "I went into the basement to get some supplies. Terrence locked me in."

"Terrence locked you in! Why did he do that?"

"He said he didn't want to put anybody else in danger," Joe answered. "He said he wants to finish this himself. I pleaded with him to let me out, but to tell you the truth, I don't think he heard a word I said."

"Any idea where he went?" Frank asked.

"Oh, yeah," Joe replied, "I know where he went. And I know who he's going to find when he gets there."

15 One Last Stunt

"If you figure on finding Antonio Lawrence there," Frank said, "then you figure wrong. I just tangled with him, and I'm convinced he's innocent."

"Innocent," Joe said. "That I don't know about. But I do know he's not the one trying to kill Terrence. That honor goes to William 'Slim Billy' Thompson."

"Slim Billy!" Frank was shocked. "How do you figure that?"

"Some clues, some hunches," Joe said, "but I'm sure I'm right. I figure he has motive: the accident during filming on *The Bridges of Rodriguez*

Ridge. Opportunity for sure: he's the safety consultant for Daredevil Fest, so he's had full access to the events. Plus I'm certain he was the pilot for the skydiving event. Terrence handed him his parachute pack. Thompson could have slit the harness while he was helping T into the pack. The skill factor is a no-brainer: he's handy with explosives, and besides being a stuntman, he was also a stunt designer, stunt coordinator, and probably a technical expert."

"So, where do we find Slim Billy?" Frank asked.

"That's the final clue," Joe replied. He described the cliff where they were to meet Thompson. "Tie this location back to the scene where his career was ended, and it says William Thompson all over it. Cliffs hold a special place in the relationship between Terrence and Thompson."

"Good work," Frank said. "But at this point, knowing who our opponent is does little to bring this to a close. He's got hostages, he's probably got Terrence by now, and he's had a whole lot of time to prepare whatever trap he's going to spring on us. This has gone from being a mystery to being a rescue operation."

"Then let's get prepared," Joe stated flatly. He jogged down the stairs to the basement. When he came back into the kitchen he was holding a long coil of rope, a grappling hook, and a lantern.

"Put these in the car," Joe said as he handed the equipment to his brother. "I've got to get one more thing."

When Joe got into the car, Frank was examining a map.

"What did you just toss in the trunk?" Frank asked.

"A little surprise," Joe replied with a grin.

"I figure we should take a different approach to the cliffs," Frank said as he traced his finger along the map. "Maybe cut down Slim Billy's advantage a bit by reaching the spot unexpectedly."

Joe took the map from his brother so Frank could start the car. "Good thinking," he said. "At this point, any little thing that shifts the initiative away from Thompson may give us the room we need to bring him down."

Frank put the car into gear. "Just remember, the stakes here are high," he said. "This lunatic has our parents and may have our friend. Don't get reckless, but if you see an opportunity to take him out, there's no need to be gentle."

"Trust me, making nice with this guy is not in the program," Joe said.

Twenty minutes later Frank eased the car to a

stop on a deserted dirt road at the base of the Hollywood Hills.

"The way I figure it," he said to Joe, "the spot where he wants us to meet is a ten-minute walk."

"Yeah, except he'll be at the top of the cliff and we'll be at the bottom."

"If I remember correctly, the hills aren't that high at the spot he wants us to meet him. Plus, we won't both be at the base of the cliff if you stick to the plan."

"I'll be in position," Joe assured his brother. "You just keep him focused on you."

The two brothers split up. Frank walked along the base of the cliff while Joe made his way up the rocks to the top. It was rough going for Joe. He was holding a large box, and Frank had purposely kept the rope and grappling hook. For their plan to work, it would be a matter of both precise timing and well-honed skill.

Frank walked for ten minutes through the darkness. He had considered using a flashlight, but decided that every step he got closer to Slim Billy without alerting the man would be precious.

Unfortunately, Slim Billy was not about to oblige Frank's wishes. Without warning, a gunshot rang out and a bullet kicked up the dirt at Frank's feet.

He must be wearing night goggles, Frank thought. He can see me, but I can't see him.

As if in answer to Frank's unspoken request, Slim Billy fired up a powerful electric lantern. He shone the beam around the top of the hill.

In silhouette Frank could see Slim Billy standing over the still body of Terrence McCauley. He could also see that the young stuntman was bound at his wrists and ankles.

As if that weren't bad enough, what Frank saw next caused him to shudder. Bound and gagged and standing shoulder to shoulder on a narrow six-inch ledge with their backs flattened against the cliff face were the three missing parents. The drop to the rocks below was only about thirty feet. But tied up as they were, if they fell they would be seriously injured if not killed outright.

"Kids today just do not listen," Slim Billy shouted. "You were all supposed to come together. Instead this joker shows up all alone," he said as he jabbed Terrence with his boot. "And now we're still one Hardy short."

"Sorry to disappoint you," Frank said.

"Well, I'll just change my plans," Slim Billy said. "First, drop that rope you're holding," he said, indicating with his revolver the equipment that Frank was carrying.

Frank let the rope drop to the ground. However, as he did so, he surreptitiously gave some slack to the end with the grappling hook.

"So what's your new plan?" Frank asked Slim Billy. If he had calculated correctly, Joe was still probably out of position. He needed to buy his brother a little time.

"Nothing too elaborate," Thompson responded. "Nothing like the traps I set up before. I think I'll just shoot poor Terrence here and then I'll trigger some explosions that'll send your folks to their graves. I'll leave you and your brother to pick up the pieces while I escape out of the country. That'll teach you to meddle in my business."

"So how did you set up your stunts?" Frank asked. "Some were absolutely brilliant." He needed to keep Thompson's attention riveted on him. An ego stroke or two could do the trick.

"Come on, none of them were all that tough," Slim Billy said.

"Humor a stupid kid like me," Frank added.

"Remote-control stuff, mostly," Slim Billy explained. "I love explosives. Bomb in the trailer refrigerator—expensive but not that hard to acquire. M-80 through the window—no problem. Okay, so trying to run you off the road in that truck I stole from Silver Lining may be a bit too straightforward, but, hey, you work with what you got.

"I cut the strap on Terrence's parachute pack and hitched small explosives to the steering and brake lines on the semi," Slim Billy continued. "The trickiest part was shooting him out of the sky with that remote-controlled airplane."

"Speaking of airplanes," Frank said. A loud buzzing sound suddenly filled the sky. Instinctively, Slim Billy took his eyes off Frank to locate the noise.

His eyes locked on Brian McCauley's model Zano 2000 just in time. Slim Billy ducked as a large, sleek model airplane came buzzing straight at his head.

Frank used the distraction to make his move. He dropped to the ground and with one fluid motion grabbed the grappling hook, rolled to his feet, and threw the steel object with pinpoint accuracy. The hook flew to the top of the cliff. One of its sharp tines cut into Slim Billy's left leg. With a mighty tug, Frank jerked the rope attached to the hook, sending Slim Billy tumbling to the ground with a shout of pain.

The injured man struggled to get to his feet. At the same time, he tried to raise his gun. However, the model airplane buzzed him once more, keeping him pinned to the ground and knocking the gun from his hand.

After using the remote control one last time to make the Zano 2000 plummet to Slim Billy's chest, Joe dropped the unit and ran up to where the villain lay. He kicked the gun out of Thompson's reach.

"Don't you just hate it when one of your own traps comes back to bite you?" Joe said, beaming as he dropped down beside Thompson. He rolled him over and put a knee into the small of the man's back. Then he used the rope that was attached to the grappling hook to bind Thompson's arms and legs together.

"Just like in the rodeo," Terrence murmured as he regained consciousness.

"How you feeling?" Joe asked as he untied his friend.

"Groggy and bruised, but I'll be okay."

"Good," Frank said as he came panting up the hill, "because this isn't over by a long shot."

16 One Last Bang

"Bad guy caught, case closed," Terrence said.

"Nope," Frank responded.

"I heard him say something about explosives," Joe added.

Terrence shook his head. "Our folks!"

"Bound and gagged on a narrow ledge with dynamite strapped to them," Frank said. "And with a perfectionist like Slim Billy, I'm betting there's a timer attached to the explosives, just in case his remote control failed."

The three young men went to the edge of the cliff and peered down into the darkness at the tops of their parents' heads.

"Get some light," Frank ordered.

Joe retrieved the flashlight that Terrence had dropped when Slim Billy knocked him out. He returned to the cliff edge and shone the beam down.

"You guys okay?" Frank asked.

"Are they okay?" Joe chuckled nervously. "They've got dynamite strapped to them."

"I meant, are they all conscious," Frank explained. He looked down at the three parents.

Each adult nodded.

"Good," Frank said. "We won't have to haul dead weight up here."

"So you have a plan?" Terrence asked.

"Yeah," Frank replied. "What you'll have to do is lower me down the side of the cliff so I have both hands free."

"You!" Terrence protested. "I'm the stuntman here. I'm going over the side."

"Nope, me," Joe said. "Terrence is too heavy."

"You're stronger than I am," Frank said to his brother. "I'd feel better if both you and Terrence held the line." Frank began to wind the rope around his waist. "Plus, there's no time to argue," he said as he tied the rope into a reliable knot.

"First thing when I'm down there, I'll disarm the explosives and then we can haul our folks up."

"Slim Billy is a genius when it comes to rigging explosives," Terrence said.

"I sure am," Thompson said from the ground. He seemed amused at the young men's predicament.

"Never mind him," Frank said. "We're going to do this just fine."

"When we lower you down," Terrence suggested, "ungag my dad first. He should be able to talk you through the process."

"Good idea," Frank said.

The three friends peered over the cliff edge once more.

"Let's do it," Frank said.

Joe and Terrence took a firm grip on the rope and braced their legs against giant boulders. "Good luck," they both said as they slowly lowered Frank over the side.

"How are you doing?" Frank asked, hanging next to Brian McCauley as he undid the gag around his mouth.

"Just dandy," the man replied, moving his jaw back and forth to get the circulation going. "Okay, let's not waste time. Work fast but carefully."

The first person Frank was to release was Mrs. Hardy. Bracing his feet against the ledge his mom was standing on, Frank removed her gag and waited for Brian McCauley's instructions.

"You see the green wire that runs from the first stick of dynamite into the timer?" he asked.

"Yeah, I see it," Frank answered.

"Good. What you need to do is lift the wire gently, but don't break it."

Frank reached for the wire.

"Wait!" Brian exclaimed. "Did you bring something to cut it with?"

Frank squeezed his hand into his back pocket. He removed his Swiss army knife and opened the wire-cutter tool.

"Good," Brian McCauley said.

"Hurry up down there," Joe shouted from atop the cliff. "Our arms are giving out."

"After I release Mom and you haul her up, I'll have a ledge to stand on."

"Get back to work," Brian directed.

Once more Frank gently lifted the green wire.

"Okay, now strip off the covering very carefully. Don't cut through the wire."

Frank did as he was instructed. When he had removed the green plastic covering he saw that the wire inside consisted of several twisted strands of copper.

"Now what?" Frank asked.

144

"Put the knife in your mouth," McCauley said. "You'll need two hands for this next step."

When both of Frank's hands were free, McCauley continued.

"Carefully separate the strands from one another. There should be five. Untwist them very carefully. Now cut the one in the middle," Brian McCauley instructed.

Frank took the knife from his mouth. He positioned it around the center wire and neatly snipped it.

Immediately, there was a noise like a clock winding down.

"Booby trap!" Brian McCauley screamed.

Frank's instincts took over. Realizing that Thompson had rigged the timer to wind down to zero if the device was tampered with, Frank simply tore the dynamite from his mom and threw it toward the rocks below.

It exploded mere feet away, the force of the blast throwing Frank into his mother and against the cliff wall.

"I'm losing my grip!" Joe screamed.

Joe and Terrence struggled to maintain their hold. Terrence swiftly wrapped the slipping rope twice around his own arm.

"Ahhh!" he screamed as the rope bit into his skin.

"I'm solid again," Joe said as he recovered his hold on the rope.

"What happened?" Frank asked Brian.

"He's got this wired up so strangely," Brian replied.

"Or he changed the wire casing colors so we'd have trouble disarming them," Frank suggested. "Why don't I just rip all of the explosives free?"

"Too dangerous," McCauley answered. "Carefully untie my hands, get topside, and then toss the rope down so your mom can be hauled up. I'll examine the device strapped to me so when you come back down to disarm it I'll know a little more."

Frank did as he was told. After his mom was safe on top of the cliff, he tied the rope back on his own waist and was once again lowered over the cliff.

"We'll need to work fast," Brian McCauley said. "We're almost out of time."

"Do his dynamite first, son," Mr. Hardy instructed after Frank removed his father's gag.

Frank knew better than to argue with his dad.

"I have this one figured out," Brian McCauley stated. "After you disarm it, get up top and send the rope back down. I'll free your dad."

Frank worked swiftly, following Brian Mc-

Cauley's instructions. The stunt coordinator was soon free from his trap.

Ten minutes later all three parents stood beside their sons and the trussed-up Slim Billy Thompson. They all sat down and rested while Joe walked out to the highway to flag down help.

Thirty minutes later, Joe returned.

"I got a passing motorist to put in a call to the police."

"Uh, could somebody at least turn me on my back?" Slim Billy asked sheepishly. "All the blood is pooling in my forehead."

"I should just throw you over the edge," Brian McCauley spat into the face of the former stuntman.

"Not necessary, Brian," Mr. Hardy said. He put a restraining hand on his friend's shoulder.

"With more than a dozen counts of attempted murder hanging over his head, I think Slim Billy will be spending the rest of his days in jail," Frank added.

"He'd better be," Terrence said. "If he thinks he was somehow paying me back for the accident that ended his stunt career, he doesn't even want to know what I'll do to him for putting our parents in danger."

"Speaking of danger," Joe said, "do you think

they'll redo Daredevil Fest now that the accidents have been cleared up?"

"I hope so," Terrence said. "If for no other reason than I won't have to hear Antonio Lawrence whine for a whole year about how he got cheated out of a chance to beat me."

"Beat *you?*" Joe laughed. "Hey, if the tournament is back on, you'll both have to worry about beating me!"

Bullying.
Threats.
Bullets.

Locker
searches?
Metal
detectors?

Fight back without fists.

MTV's Fight For Your Rights: Take A Stand Against Violence can give you the power to find your own solutions to youth violence. Find out how you can take a stand in your community at FightForYourRights.MTV.com.

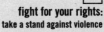

fight for your rights:
take a stand against violence

Split-second suspense...
Brain-teasing puzzles...

No case is too tough for the world's greatest teen detective!

NANCY DREW®

MYSTERY STORIES

By Carolyn Keene

Join Nancy and her friends in
thrilling stories of adventure and intrigue

Look for brand-new mysteries
wherever books are sold

Available from Minstrel® Books
Published by Pocket Books

2313

Todd Strasser's
AGAINST THE ODDS™

Shark Bite
The sailboat is sinking, and Ian just saw the
biggest shark of his life.

Grizzly Attack
They're trapped in the Alaskan wilderness
with no way out.

Buzzard's Feast
Danger in the desert!

Gator Prey
They know the gators are coming for
them...it's only a matter of time.

 A MINSTREL® BOOK
Published by Pocket Books   2023